PRESENCE

PRESENCE

Mysterium Tremendum of Manila`s Messiah

To Andrew,
I hope that
you enjoy this.
Ken.

KEN EVANS

authorHOUSE®

AuthorHouse™
1663 Liberty Drive
Bloomington, IN 47403
www.authorhouse.com
Phone: 1-800-839-8640

Published by AuthorHouse 10/05/2012

ISBN: 978-1-4772-3788-5 (sc)
ISBN: 978-1-4772-3789-2 (e)

PRESENCE

A presence that disturbs me with joy
Of elevated thoughts: a sense sublime
Of something far more deeply interfused,
Whose dwelling is the light of setting suns.

William Wordsworth

PREFACE

MANILA, Manifesting, Mysterious, Messianic, Machiavellian, and mad, maggoty, magisterial, magnanimous, meandering. muddled, malarial, mawkish, multicoloured, man-eating, merciful, melancholic, magnetic, maudlin, malignant, malodorous, mendacious, mercantile, mephitic, mesmeric, metaphysical, murky, meandering, musing, meteoric, migratory, masquerading, melodramatic, misrepresented, musical, musing, mythical, makeshift, metropolis at the middle of my minds eye.

MANILA, the eternal feminine city of the East, mothering her twenty million souls and a hundred thousand Jeepneys flowing in perpetual motion along her smoking highways, while beneath her feet the neglected esteros festering with human effluence.

MANILA, caught in the ebb and flow of history, at one time a kingdom in her own right, a land of gold, and already a wondrous place long before the Spaniards arrived. Destined to become my `Serenissima of the Orient`, an elegant heart-land, criss-crossed with (esteros) canals easing the flooding of the metropolis during rainy seasons, and besides providing elegant forms of transportation, beautifying the city, creating a veritable Venice of the East. With its cherished dream of beautiful Esteros, along which the wealthy would be transported languidly in gondola-style opulence.

Imagine this Dear Reader, Manila in its hey-day, the banks of the thirty-five or so Esteros, their banks elegantly lined with polished sandstone, and with English style pavements, and rows of tall white wood and stone built houses with huge awnings standing back from the canal banks, creating views reminiscent of classical European cities. Hence these canals enjoyed the protection of the City Guardians—men of substance, until finally they became the main democratised commercialised routes for carrying ordinary goods from the provinces and suburbs into the increasingly densely populated areas of Quiapo and Divisoria.

From this time forward Manila the elegant city went into material and spiritual decline!

PROLOGUE

To Manila's government officials and wealthy businessmen, the phalanx of shanty slum-dwellings, suspended like a narrow enclosed bridge on its rickety bamboo scaffolding, running along the left bank of San Juan canal, a mere stones—throw from the highly-cherished Quiapo church, had been declared an `Eyesore and a Public Disgrace`. But to its one thousand or so `squatter-population; young and old, it is their home they `half-jokingly` call "Babylon"—the beautiful place, reminiscent of its biblical sister which once dwelt on the banks of the Euphrates.

But the Estero San Juan is no longer the beautiful elegant flowing waterway it once had been; but now a dank stagnant cess-pit with a stench as oppressive as its offensive appearance. No-one was sure when the shanty-dwellings had been built, for like so many other encampments which have taken root on any empty spare patch of ground in Manila, it had one morning quite suddenly appeared, emerging little by little as the Babylonians themselves tell, first as a precarious single lodging-place, which like a slender water-snake, would grow each night to become a serpentine structure, little more than a metre wide but more than a kilometre in length, from head to tail.

Externally, along its length it resembles a long thin bizarre patchwork tapestry of recycled building materials; of rusting corrugated roofing sheets, wooden pallets, flattened cardboard packing cases, transparent and coloured polythene sheeting, and anything else that would cover a hole, all cleverly woven into a single canvas overlooking the stagnant waters of the San Juan Estero. And when by-passers smell these fetid waters they assume that the inhabitants who occasionally peered out at them from tiny window-holes would be tainted by this bubbling cauldron of human waste and trash. But no amount of imagination would lead them to visualise it`s seductive interior homeliness and sense of community, or its inhabitant's sensibilities.

From inside it resembles a long narrow passage way fashioned from a series of rooms, connected but not continuous, because the impression is that each successive room is simply an extension of the previous one, making the floor of each one, at a slightly different level, and never completely flat, but with gradients and sometimes flexible areas which move when walked upon. But most importantly, although externally all is dross of the worst sort, the thin walls are a boundary between one world and another, for within all is clean; spotlessly clean! The overall impression to any stranger would be that it is suspended by rubber cables and constantly but gently in motion, bouncing gently up and down and swinging from side to side, undulating like a meandering Chinese dancing dragon during Chinese New

Year! Yet perhaps it is more organic than this, because of its vaporous heat more like actually being inside the body of a living dragon, very hot during the day, and still warm and moist throughout the night.

Within this body more than a thousand citizens: children, parents, and cousins and aunties, all refugees from the Provinces, deftly move in and out of their tiny annex-like rooms, sliding and ducking in between each other, as if performing a gentle elegantly choreographed dance, cooking and eating and sleeping, and acting out all of the essential movements of daily living. Not silently, for there is a perpetual hum of voices and human activities and smells, and aromas of warm bodies and food and deodorants.

Outside are several doorways of sorts, openings along its length connected to the street by small bridges, some with recycled doors from demolished buildings, and others with woven bamboo sections, which hang like stiff curtains. In between these entrances here and there are small apertures and widows of varying sizes and at different heights which are lost in the overall patch-work appearance of dazzling colours and varying textures. To any alien adult visitor it would appear to be a long straggling shanty hut, but to any child from afar, raised on any fantasy stories of Disney-Land it would be completely magical, breaking all the laws of conventional town architecture and appearances of ordinary dwellings.

It was here, within this suspended village that our story begins, or should I say where I have chosen to start telling it, for in fact this story has existed since the beginning of time and will continue to re-occur eternally, one way or another, almost down to its tiniest detail.

CHAPTER 1

One wet September afternoon one of the small children, playing alone in a small room, with her tiny wind-up clockwork plastic toy doll, watched as it walked determidley towards a small hole in the floor in the corner of the room, fall and disappear down into the stagnant canal water beneath the room. She heard it plop and instantly knew how to retrieve it using a piece of plastic hose pipe with a bent wire hook taped to one end, having observed many occasions how all of her brothers and sisters, and other grown-ups had successfully `fished` things out of the fetid water; and lying full-length on the floor she gently lowered the piece of hose through the hole and into the water below, moving it to and fro. The swirling wire hook dislodged fragments of rotting paper and torn strips of coloured polythene floating on the surface, as she stirred the waters, she then froze in terror at the sight of something resembling a human face, a pale lean unshaven face, with partly closed eyes staring into hers, glistening in the grey water below.

In her panic she screamed and letting go of the piece of hose, was immediately surrounded by the other children, who scrambled to gain access to the small hole. One by one they took their turn to peer into the shadows and the detritus below them. The water was placidly still with a thick layer of floating rotting litter, and as each took their turns to see, each child in turn was overcome by the same sense of panic and fear. Soon there were others; bigger brothers, and parents who squinted through the hole, checking the sludge below for the face. Some disagreed, saying that it was face-shaped, but not a face, but others were already in the water beneath the room, trying to clear the body of the floating congealed trash that had already formed a skin of pulped waste, embracing the body like a garish loose-fitting garment.

Several eager to help youths hurriedly manoeuvred the naked body to the canal bank, and sluiced it with clean water, and lifted it into an old blanket, which they used as a kind of first-aid stretcher, and carried it, still dripping grey water, into the nearest passage-way inside the apartments. There was no sign of breathing, but the body was still pink and warm and perhaps alive, and there was almost an indistinct heartbeat. They pulled the blanket around the body as if wrapping it in a shroud, partly out of respect for its nakedness, but also to cover the several wounds that had been inflicted on it.

In almost no time the whole village had become aware that something was happening and began converging on the small passage. Children were excitedly running up and down; some squealing with a mixture fear and pleasure others crying, without knowing the reason why.

Despite being an unofficial and unregistered residence, the place they called Babylon was organised as one, with its own elected Barangay Captain and Councillors and even its own private volunteer police force, complete with uniforms and badges. For a while all was mayhem, children shrieking and parents haranguing one another as they expressed a variety of opinions; everyone eager to catch a glimpse of the drowned man, until the large bulky shape of Ma Theresa Dela Cruz, the ever-present Councillor and wife of the Barangay Captain pressed her way through the packed mob surrounding the body, bringing both silence and order to the scene. She was known to all simply as `Ma`, a contraction of her first name-Mary, but also because she was like a mother to everyone, and was mum-shaped, but still prettily attractive.

The lifeless body was lying on the floor wrapped as if in a shroud with only his sad face exposed. Ma. Theresa questioned the youths who had retrieved it and carried it inside.

"Had anybody seen you? Was anybody watching? Had there been any life in the body?"

She was not sure what other questions to ask. Her concern had been to settle things down until she could get some idea what to do with it. In the meantime she instructed the youths to put the corpse in the tiny empty room, which sometimes served as an occasional bed-spacers room, and place the body on the old dilapidated bamboo bed there, and to cover it completely with the old blanket. And then she reminded everyone that the incident was a Council matter, and that in the meantime, it was Council Business, which meant that it was something not to be discussed outside the Village. They were all aware of this anyway, knowing that the authorities were ever out to use any reason to force their closure.

Although most of the Babylonians were poor, a dispossessed people as they wished to say, there were some who were professionally qualified teachers and nurses, and even a few attorneys of sorts. And hearing the hullabaloo some of the nurses had already hastened to the small room to offer their services, trying to convince Ma. Theresa that they at least should check to see if there were any signs of life, and any chances of resuscitation. It was no easy task, for Ma. Theresa took her responsibilities seriously, and she imagined the reprimands she would receive from the other Councillors if she made a wrong decision, but finally she agreed that the nurses should at least check the body for signs of life.

It was getting dark and there was no electricity in the small room and the three nurses took it in turns to hold the flash-light while each in turn listened and tested for signs of a pulse. They immediately realised that the body was not that of a Filipino. It was too long and lean for that, and very pale, undernourished even. With wounds on the chest and tears in the skin, a swollen and bruised face, with a prominent nose and several days growth on the chin and upper lip: the eyes partially open, and the lips pursed as if forming unspoken words. The body was neither cold nor warm, and in this sense neither dead nor alive, but in a half-way state of perhaps suspended animation.

They checked and re-checked the pulse, and with stethoscopes listened for signs of breath, and checked every inch of the body for signs of life. The hands were open, displaying what appeared to be bullet-wounds to each palm, a small hole in the middle of the inside of each hand, and a massive torn wound on the back. It was the same with the feet, they too had been shot through at close-range, leaving a ragged hole in the soles. In the semi-darkness the three nurses whispered their fears that the man must have been a victim of a sinister ritual killing, a brutal punishment for something, but they could not understand that there were no other signs of a coupe de grace, no sign of a final fatal wound to the back of the head! They turned the body over, revealing a scourged back, a criss-cross pattern of deep lacerations from the shoulders to the waist caused by a hooked instrument of some sort, intended to cause maximum pain, and a slow death.

Despite the depth of some of the lacerations there were already signs of healing, with scabs forming across the shoulders. They agreed that the best they could do was to bathe the body, perhaps as part of preparation for burial. Starting with the feet, they carefully cleaned the wounds and bound them with strips of linen torn from an old bed-sheet, its whiteness offering a small sign of their concern and respect for this broken body. Next the legs and the abdomen were bathed and patted dry, as if tending a baby, and the torn torso rubbed with the only sweet-smelling unguent available, a cheap perfumed moisturising cream, which they hoped would hold back the smell of death. And then finally the head and face. The eyes were still partly open; enough to see that the pupils were grey or pale blue.

"Perhaps he was an American?" One of the nurses said.

"Maybe, but the nose is big, . . . maybe an Arab ?"

The third, who had said almost nothing up to this point, stood back and moved the flash-light full on the cadaver's face.

"He is too thin for Mericano, . . . smells too sweet for an Arab, even though he`s been in the water some time, . . . and too handsome for Chinese, . . . probably about thirty I`d say, . . . and also circumcised, . . . did you notice ?"

They briefly chortled, but there was a childish embarrassment in their laughter.

Finally they combed his long dark hair, and listened once more for signs of breath. There was none, they all agreed, but without saying anything, they tidied the small room as if there was life there still, as if they might be alerted by some small sign, for the surface of the body was still flexible and warm and moist.

There was only an old torn faded curtain to close off the room from the narrow passage-way, and waiting outside were Ma. Theresa and her husband, the Barangay Captain, and some of the other Councillors. They had already discussed the body, and its arrival and what they should do about it. They all looked in at the body. Pepe, the smallest of the councillors, a short weedy man, quickly blurted out that the body was not dead, and that just because there was no movement, this meant nothing.

Ma. Theresa thanked the nurses, and suggested that there was nothing else anyone could do at this time of the evening and that the Council would decide things in the morning.

This is what Ma. Theresa had understood after the quick short meeting after her husband had arrived home from dealing with other matters that evening, but nobody wanted to sleep on it, and the small group drifted along to the `barungay office`; a sad little room at the far end of the long tunnel of many rooms to settle their nerves with `shots` of cheap rum and to speculate on their latest problem.

The barungay council was a variable sized committee of never fewer than four, but occasionally as many as twenty or so, especially when organising fiestas and celebrations, baptisms, marriages, funerals and beauty competitions. But on this occasion there were five. Besides Ma. Theresa, there was John, Ma. Theresa`s husband the Barangay Captain, a tall thin serious man who had spent most of his married life working far from home, as a Forester, and who in his wife`s imagination had grown to resemble the tall trees he had worked among. Nobody ever used his first name, even his wife. He was to everyone simply the Barangay Captain. And there was Geronimo, a gentle and softly-spoken ex-security guard, Mario an excitable odd-job man, able to fix more or less anything, Mark-Anthony (whose father had great expectations of his dilettante son) and Pepe, a small wiry farm-worker from the North, and one-time helot. Together they were more like brothers and considerably more able to settle community matters than most local official councillors.

Each of them had already speculated on the possibilities of how the body had come to be caught up in the debris beneath the village. Occasionally swollen bodies of dead dogs and cats, and cat-sized rats had been caught in the bamboo scaffolding which held the village aloft, but never before a human corpse. The stagnant canal water was usually lifeless and still, but the rains had stopped only as few weeks before, and there was at least a little movement in the estero, and possibly the body could have drifted beneath the congealed putrid lumpy skin of rotting debris, which was sometimes more that a foot thick. But this would have taken perhaps more than a week, by which time the body would have been decomposing! On the other hand it seemed more likely that the body had been thrown beneath the tangled scaffolding, or even planted there for a purpose.

The small barangay office furniture consisted of two roughly upholstered, but torn bench seats, a large chair for the barangay captain and a small desk; they sat according to their perceived rank, Pepi at the small end of the bench.

Mark, who preferred to be addressed as Marcus initiated the meeting.

"We need to be careful, . . . I had a feeling that something like this would happen sometime." His voice quavering.

The others concurred, nodding and sipping their cheap Tanduay rum. The Barangay Captain searched their faces, trying to read the seriousness in their expressions.

"It`s possible, that some of our enemies planted the body there, and are waiting to see what we will do, . . . but which of our enemies? . . . that`s the problem !"

Everyone in the village understood that whatever was outside was a threat to their survival, and that their main enemies were several powerful politicians, the City mayor and his cronies, the big bosses at City Hall, and the Business Bosses, who operated the high-rise modern buildings which overshadowed them. And also probably some of the surrounding Barangay chiefs, who were jealous because the villagers lived a free life, paying no taxes. Pepe suggested that if the body had been planted, it would not have been tortured, and that it would have probably been the body of a girl not a man, perhaps one of the prostitutes who hang around Quiapo church.

Their investigations and suggestions circulated, round and round in tempo with the movement of the Tanduay bottle and eventually spiralled out of the realms of practical possibilities. Their conclusions before they left to go to their beds were, that anything was possible, that the body was not that of a Pinoy, and most likely a gangland execution, simply dumped there under cover of night, because there were no street lights. And that what they would do with the body was a matter for a further meeting! And with that decision, they went to their beds.

CHAPTER 2

The following morning the village was unusually quiet as if everyone, including the children had sensed a sadness that had settled over the village; the news of the previous day had not yet penetrated every corner of each and every small room, but as children bathed, and mothers prepared breakfast, and bigger brothers and sisters returned from their errands with pandesol and cooked noodles from the road sellers, they caught snippets of tsismis that a drowned man had been rescued, or that somebody had been shot, or other desperate tragedies had already brought bad luck on the village.

One of the three nurses from the night before, who had checked the body for signs of life had woken early from a bad dream, and had hurried to the small room where the body had been left. She had dreamt that the man had visited her during the night and had showed her his wounds, and asked her bind them with ointment and bandages. As she arranged the hands across the chest, she felt a small movement, a kind of resistance in the arms, perhaps a sign of life. While she was cleaning the wounds, the other two nurses arrived, and she told them of her dream and how the man had spoken to her, and instructed her to bind his wounds with myrrh.

Although there was still no movement, there were none of the usual signs of death; no rigor mortis or cold stiffness, but there was no heartbeat or sign of breathing either. They were puzzled, but tended to the body as if expecting something to happen. Others passing through the narrow passageway stopped and called in asking if there was any hope, and crossed themselves, and promised to light a candle during the day, and whispered a prayer, and Ma. Theresa stopped by and asked the nurses if there was anything needed from the pharmacy. After the nurses had attended to the four wounds, they covered the body with a clean linen sheet, and pulled the patchwork curtain across the opening as a sign of respect for his modesty.

During the day some of the seniors who rarely went out, visited the small room, either out of respect for the dead, or curiosity. Young children also pushed their heads through the opening to make sure that the dead man would not be lonely. And finally he was visited by the whole Barangay Council and village volunteer chief of police, the Barangay Captains family, and one of the Villagers who was also a Knight of St. John, and a server at the lesser Basilica of San Sebastian. It had been suggested that someone who handled the Blessed Sacrament might, perhaps endow some grace, which might just edge the lifeless body over the boundary between life and death. Marcus Antonius quipped that resurrection would be more likely if his visitors had come from the local Girlie Bar, and boasted that he had someone in mind. There were a few chuckles, but Ma. Theresa promised her prayers for that purpose later that day, and the Barangay Captain set about the business of enquiring about missing persons and possible suicides and murder victims.

During the afternoon one of the women who worked at Quiapo market brought one of her close friends to see the body, he was a helot, a quack doctor who sold herbal medicines outside the church and also knew about embalming, and he had suggested massaging the body with frankincense oil, in case the man's soul should leave without any blessings. The pale yellow oil with its rich fragrance brought life to the room and dignity to the corpse. Another neighbour placed a crucifix on his chest, and small votive candles were set either side of the bed. Sampaguita necklaces were laid on his head like a crown of tiny pearls, and his dried lips were anointed with camphor. By the evening the room resembled a small shrine, with flowers, and rosary beads and prayer cards, and the shrouded body smelling of incense, illuminated by the thin moonlight struggling through the tiny square window above the bed.

The small room became the focus of the evening's gathering; some of the villagers who returned from their jobs brought in more flowers as a gift for the man, and hung around gossiping about minor miracles they had heard about during the day. They speculated on the man`s identity and the possible reasons he had arrived at their place instead of any other place. It was unnecessary to attempt to analyse these matters, but common sense decreed that nothing ever happened without a reason, and the reason must be either good or bad. And if he wasn't a Filipino, and not an Americano, then he might be a Nazareno ! None of them were able to fathom how they had reached this conclusion, but it had an intuitive ring of truth about it in its obviousness, and its matter-of-factness, and therefore its truthfulness.

These speculations continued deep into the night; those who became exhausted by the tsismis drifted away to their abodes and their beds in the long snake-like tunnel that was Babylon, suspended on bamboo stilts above the dark canal swaying and creaking in the moonlight. And others who had not yet satisfied their appetite for news and the sustenance of gossip congregated around the tiny sepulchre. But just at the point of their last `goodnights` as they prepared to depart for their rooms, a small rattling sound came from the still body. There was no movement, but the shaft of moonlight piecing the window had sharpened and now illuminated the serene features of his thin sad face. They held their breath and listened, something stirred, perhaps there was shallow breathing, and they could hear it, like a distant wind from somewhere far away. Ma. Theresa, who had heard the prayers, quickly appeared, crossed herself and recited the `Ave`, the others followed suite and recited well-remembered familiar prayers; they wanted to leave him and go to their beds but they could not move. Ma. Theresa suggested an all night vigil, she could feel it she said, someone was speaking to her, and it was an obligation.

Nobody moved, and they all knelt in the semi-darkness, taking it in turns to begin another prayer, another request for the man's life, for his redemption, and even if he had already died, for his resurrection. They prayed and begged, and promised that they would try harder to follow the commandments, and honour each other's supplications'.

The quiet prayers continued intermittently for the rest of the night, and ended as the sun came up, sending shafts of brilliant sunlight through the many small holes in the rusted corrugated roofing sheets. They could hear their neighbours taking their baths and cooking breakfast, and the vapours of coffee mingling with pungent smells of fried dry fish and soap, and one by one they drifted away to attend to their families and prepare for the new day.

CHAPTER 3

While Ma. Theresa was attending to the needs of the spirit, her husband's concerns were on the earthly matters of the `body's identity and how it had arrived beneath the village. He had checked at all of the local police depots, and at the hospital, the newsrooms, at the City Hall, and in the bars, but there had been no reported missing persons, or gang-fights, or unresolved cases of shooting incidents. But this did not rule out the possibility of a `set-up`, which had been his main suspicion from the start.

His second worry, already discussed with the other Councillors, was the disposal of the remains, a thought which had troubled him more than he had been willing to admit. One of the Councillors had suggested that they could quietly slip it back in the canal further along from the village, and leave it for someone else to find, or bury it in a distant location in the province; but his conscience held him back and besides, his wife had several times hinted that there might be a hidden purpose.

Ma. Theresa had been thinking similar thoughts. During the night she had woken up and been unable to sleep, and her movements and softly-whispered prayers woke her husband. There was no light in their small room, but their closeness included a kind of second-sight when chatting to each other in the dark.

"Are you worried?" He asked her.

"No husband, . . . but I can really feel something, . . . there`s a purpose in this, . . . I know it husband."

"Perhaps!" He said.

"So why don`t you feel something too husband?"

The Barangay Captain had been expecting this kind of interrogation sooner or later. He knew his wife`s sensitivity, and the many times she had felt something which neither could explain but which inevitably turned out to have been real. When she spoke like that he knew he had to listen and not oppose her.

He replied.

"So what do we do now ? That's our problem, . . . He`s not properly dead or alive, . . . and his wounds, . . . if someone had wanted to kill him, . . . It only needs a shot to the head, . . . one shot . . . why would they need to torture him, . . . There`s lots of things that don`t add up, . . . who knows . . ."

He heard her swallow hard in the dark silence, and knew that she had been waiting for the dawn and had been crying, and knew also that she would already have imagined the several possibilities of how the man had died, and also some of the possible reasons for his arrival beneath their village.

"God knows." She said resolutely.

The Barangay Captain`s mind shifted hastily from one image to another; he saw the grey face peering up at him as through the eyes of the child who had first discovered it, and the pale yellow glow of the dead face in the whispish moonbeam the night before, and the bandaged hands and feet, and the sad face, not of a Pinoy and not of a crook, not an angry face, somehow not even the face of a real man, but sculptured, with prominent cheekbones, a kind face bearing a wearied expression, a face he somehow knew but dare not acknowledge.

"You know he moved last night, don`t you ?" She ventured.

"I heard that, but somehow, . . . is it be true ?"

Ma. Therese's thoughts were also in full flow; there was a purpose, of this she was sure, and she thought first about her own troubles and then the difficulties that had caused the many recent meetings of the Barangay council; of the threats to dismantle the village by City Hall, false accusations from the Police department; of breaking every conceivable by-law; of the village running a vice-ring, illegal gambling, prostitution, procuring illegal abortions, on and on and on, her mind swung from one threat to another.

"Husband, did you know I always pray for someone or something to help us, . . ."

He reached out with his hand to touch her and replied softly.

"I know it my sweet wife, . . . and God is always listening to you . . ."

CHAPTER 4

As soon as the sun came up Ma. Theresa felt an uncontrollable compulsion to see the body again, sleeping but not yet dead, for she had already decided that there was hope, and she hurried along to the small room. As she drew-back the curtain, she had been expecting to see some further signs of life, but the flowers from the previous day had already wilted, and the burnt-down candles had left an impression of defeat which saddened her. She closed the curtain behind her and spoke softly to the man.

"I know you can hear me, . . . just give me a sign, . . . so the others can see, . . . it`s hard here, . . . you bring us hope, . . ."

She wanted to kneel and pray, but she also wanted to do something that would stir life into his still body. She grasped his hand and noticed a tiny blood-stain on the bandage, which had obviously just issued from the wound, it was fresh blood whereas before there had been nothing.

This was her sign, she checked the other hand and both feet, and yes, there was blood, small spots of fresh blood, the sure sign of mortality! She wanted to shout out and bring everyone to see it: he was alive and somehow she had convinced herself in the space of a few seconds of thought that she had known all along; and began clearing the dying flowers and burnt-out candles from the room.

She hurried back to her husband.

“Husband! There`s fresh blood coming from his wounds, he`s bleeding, . . . So he must be alive, . . . Can a dead man bleed?”

The Barangay Captain was drying his body after taking a quick bath, and had been thinking about other matters, but he quickly dressed and accompanied his wife to the small room.

“You are right, . . . its fresh, . . . , we have to bathe him, . . . and clean his wounds, . . . , and, . . . perhaps there`s hope.”

One of the nurses came and between them they washed the body, and whilst doing so they noticed other signs; the swollen hands and feet had lost their puffiness, and the facial expression appeared gentler, more welcoming somehow! They turned the body on its side and bathed the torn skin and ugly slashed wounds, and gently applied the myrrh ointment. It had a bitter and spicy aroma which brought tears to their eyes with its pungency.

"This will make his blood move." The nurse said, working on the hands and feet.

Ma. Theresa washed his hair, combed it carefully and attended to his face.

"Does he remind you of someone?" She asked the nurse.

It was obvious what she had in mind, for the features were clearly not those of a Filipino, but were somewhere between Southern European and Middle Eastern, Italian or Spanish perhaps, or Semitic. The nurse drew back as if to emphasise her careful judgement, tilting her head trying to view the face from several angles.

"Well! I suppose a bit like . . . but I dare`nt say, it`s a mystery! ".

She said, slightly amazed at what she imagined already to be a `blasphemy`, knowing that to think something is tantamount to doing it.

For a moment together, they stood silently looking at the `Holy face`, both moved by their own thoughts and the shared experience and the admission that this was perhaps miraculous; not just any man's body but eventfully and purposefully, and moved by the thought that it was happening here, of all possible places, in this despised dank place, an illegal squatters` slum!

"No need to say!" Ma. Theresa replied. "I was frightened even to think it, . . . , yesterday I kept looking at the images in the church, and wondering, and hoping, and praying, . . .

and my thoughts were, . . . too shameful to think these things, . . . but my girl, . . . Connie, . . . She keeps asking me that, . . . and I told her, . . . I did`nt know, . . . But really I know, . . . all along, . . . I knew, . . . we can all see it, . . ."

The nurse nodded and said nothing, but finished binding the hands and feet, and knew also that the body was now alive, although without any apparent pulse or breathing. She placed the hands on the chest and covered the body once again with a clean white bed-sheet.

Ma. Theresa clicked her fingers, in response to a sudden idea.

"I was thinking, that we should tell a priest about this, . . . maybe he would have a special prayer, . . . or maybe he would chastise us ?"

It was a question that had gone round and round in her mind from the start. Would a priest want to know about this? She had her doubts without knowing why, all she knew was that if this was a miracle, the bishops and the high priests would take it from them, would claim it as theirs, or deny it. But if this was a true miracle, then surely God would want everybody to know it? But how was she to know what to do or say to anyone, especially as her husband and the other councillors who had agreed to keep it secret?

A plan was forming in her mind. She would attend mass that morning, and would receive the communion wafer in her hand and pretend to eat it, but she would bring it back and give it to the body and touch his mouth with it. Nobody would know or suspect anything; she was respected as a regular and devout worshipper, and well-known to all the clergy. Even if it was forbidden by the Church, to carry the sacrament away, she felt satisfied that it would be permitted in these special circumstances; even the priests said that almost anything is permitted in certain circumstances, and these, she thought, were `certain` circumstances.

Together with the nurse they tidied the room, placed several vases of fresh flowers around the bed, and left the resting body in peace.

CHAPTER 5

Ma. Theresa's plan went well. She stood for a while praying by the holy image of the Black Nazarene at the rear of the church, contemplating how she would close her hand after receiving the wafer, and how she would transfer it into a clean tissue, and carry it in her hand back to the waiting body. She moved slowly down the aisle towards the priest who was delivering the sacrament, and standing before him with her cupped hands outstretched, took the wafer and moved it towards her mouth, and secretly transferred it to the tissue in her jacket pocket. She felt uneasy going out of the church, but kept her hand in her pocket in case pick-pockets might attempt stealing it from her, and hurried back to the village.

She walked up the small bridge-like gangway into her home, the four compact rooms, and immediately went into the small sepulchre and opened the folded tissue, and holding the consecrated wafer between her finger and thumb she held it above the man`s mouth, quietly saying.

"This is your body which has been given to us, . . . Eat, . . . And we shall be healed."

Ma. Theresa`s hand was shaking as she touched the lips of the man with the host, hoping and expecting something to happen, but with a feeling of deep dread. There was no movement in the body, but a growing awareness of a shared tranquillity; his face had lost its sadness and appeared to her to be bathed in a blissful serenity. Although part of her knew that the gentle mouth would not miraculously open and draw the holy wafer inside.

Without thinking of what she was doing she pulled back the sheet, and placed the wafer on his naked chest above his sacred heart and tucked in the sheet above his shoulders, and quickly returned to her small kitchen to prepare lunch. Her thoughts were about mysteries and miracles and she decided not to say anything to anyone about what she had done that morning.

She had been expecting her daughter to come home early from college, and began cooking sufficient fish and vegetables for all the family, including her two sons, waiting for them all to arrive. Both were adults and working occasionally at a small boat-yard, painting and repairing boats, and both had girl-friends; hopefully future wives. Eventually they all arrived together, excitedly asking about the body and what was happening, but she said nothing and smiled and gently tried to change the subject, but they could see that she was unusually quiet.

Connie, whose baptismal name was Concepción, was nearly eighteen, and whilst they all ate their lunch they chatted about her next birthday celebrations, and her forth-coming high-school graduation ceremony and her growing army of admirers, and her academic success, and her apparent disinterest in fashionable clothes; the list went on and on. It was true that she had many admirers and was generally acknowledged as the best looking girl in the Village, and also the smartest and the quietest. Even outside the Village complete strangers would often suddenly gaze at her and stop her, comparing her to one celebrity or another; and occasionally she would be asked for her autograph, taking all of this uninvited attention and interest as pointless curiosity.

Peter, her eldest brother, particularly enjoyed teasing her about possible boy-friends and about her over zealous dedication to her studies.

"Ma, did you know there`s a long line of gwapo guys, stretching along the whole length of the road, . . . Can`t you just wave to them, bring a bit of joy in their sad lives ?"

He threw a wicked glance at his brother, Johnny the younger one, who had flamboyantly started counting on his fingers.

"Fourteen, fifteen, sixteen, . . . Who`s gonner be lucky Sis ? . . . Why not have a birthday, graduation, and wedding all at once Sis ? . . . save money, . . . Save effort, make Mom an Dad happy, . . . have a grand-child, . . . get them a son-in-law, maybe a banker, a lawyer, maybe some rich dude, . . ."

Connie ignored them and their usual playful teasing, but she knew both of them were curious about possible boy friends, knowing also that most of her friends were going steady, but that she, most of the time, avoided dating or even casual friendship with any guys.

"There`s a time for everything," She replied, looking at her Mom for support.

"How bout the body Mom?" Johnny asked loudly.

Ma. Theresa had tried to divert their interest.

"We bathed him again today, . . . and do you know his body is still warm, and the colour of his skin pink ?"

Connie looked up from her plate, and asked.

"But is he breathing, . . . is there a pulse ?"

She waited for a reply which was slow in coming.

"Not quite, but this morning his wounds were bleeding, . . . the blood was fresh !"

The two brothers looked at each other, raising their eyebrows, and avoiding eye-contact with their Mom and sister. For a few moments nothing was said, and then Connie asked.

"So is it OK if I go and see him now, . . . Maybe I`m the only one who has`nt yet seen him !"

"Later !" Ma. Theresa said. "We will all go and see him later."

But the rest of the afternoon was filled with other things to do. There were more threatening letters from City Hall to reply to, notices of Court proceedings for littering in Public places, attorneys` instructions, letters from schools about Dengue fever, parents who needed to borrow money, stories from worried wives of Jeepney drivers who had lost their driving licence for minor traffic transgressions, invitations to talent contests, invitations to; weddings, to re-unions, to funerals, to Born-Again rally's, and invitations to see the latest blockbuster, to political meetings, to get free Dental check-ups, to Luneta Park for afternoon picnics.

CHAPTER 6

On the third day he opened his eyes; they were shocking blue!

Very early in the morning, before most of the Village was awake, one small girl who had been imploring him to wake up, screamed in terror as his eye-lids slowly opened, revealing not black or brown but to her the impossibility of blue eyes. Several mothers hurriedly congregated around the open doorway, to witness the miracle of `blue eyes`. Other children ran up and down between the phalanx of tiny apartments chanting and shouting, "Alive, Alive, Alive !" The Barangay Captain, and his wife accompanied by some of the councillors hurriedly came to survey the situation, someone brought water, and although his eyes were open, there were still no other body movements. Water was spooned into his mouth by one of the mothers, and his face was sponged down, and his arms and hands were massaged in desperation to cajole the flickering signs of life to articulate his limbs. They prayed in desperation, calling on all the saints real and unreal for his survival, trusting in God`s promise of eternal life. They understood that they still needed to do more to restore him completely to the land of the living. To generate more spiritual energy, through signs and prayer to pull him back from death's door, and that this first sign of life was a token of their faith and that in some mysterious way he had now become part of their wider family.

Ma. Theresa waited until the excitement subsided and she was at last alone with the awakened body. His eyes were open and his eye-lids flickering in the bright morning sunlight. Her thoughts were on the communion wafer; and she folded the sheet back expecting to be able to remove it, but it was not there, it had gone. She checked around his body, imagining that someone had taken it during the night, or possibly it had been eaten by rats, but there had been no signs that the sheet had been moved from how she had left it the previous day. Then she noticed a small round mark on his chest, like a faint birth-mark. It was in the right place, the exact spot where she had placed the wafer. She looked closely; the circular spot of darkened skin bore a faint image of a tiny chalice, an exact copy of the embossed image on every communion wafer. Then she understood what had happened, the wafer had miraculously been absorbed by the heat of his body, and actually had truly become His flesh. She couldn't understand how this had happened, only that it had happened, and she also knew it was the sign she had waited for.

She felt a surge of excitement and panic at the thought that she had witnessed a miracle, and whilst she was tidying the room, Connie her daughter sidled into the tiny room.

"I could`nt wait any longer", she gasped, "now that he is alive, . . . Mom, . . . is there anything I can do to help ?"

Ma. Theresa sensed awkwardness in her daughter; her eyes went back and forth between her daughter's face and that of the stranger and noticed what she thought was a similarity in both their expressions, a look of recognition, and of familiarity; they seemed to be following each others eyes.

"This seems impossible". Ma. Theresa said, "But its true, . . . it`s really happened, . . . he has come back, . . . and it happened here, . . . of all places, . . . here in our humble place, . . . who would believe this ?"

Connie edged closer to the bed and gently stroked the reclining figure's arm and forehead, knowingly looking into his face.

"Moma, . . . his head is hot, . . . like a fever, . . . and his chest Moma, . . . He`s breathing Moma, . . . not deeply, . . . and there`s breath, I know it."

"Yes". Ma. Theresa said, "He`s really here now, . . . really with us, . . . I am thinking now, . . . that someone should be here all the time, . . . in case he needs something, . . . stay here, . . . while I go and buy, . . . We can take it in turns !"

Ma Theresa brought in a chair for Connie, and wedged it between the bed and the plywood wall.

"We will take it in turns ". Ma. Theresa said, and hurried out into the passage-way.

Connie sat huddled in the small space beneath the tiny window, contemplating the strangeness of sitting so close to someone unknown to herself and to others in the village. She quietly observed the lines of his face and the faint pulse of his heart-beat, and then found herself uttering brief words of encouragement; and later still, after a while she spoke as though conversing, unravelling the story of his arrival and the story of her own life.

She spoke softly. She introduced herself.

"I`m Connie, and you are our friend now, . . . we are all poor here so I can`t understand why you called—in here, . . . particularly?"

Connie readjusted the curtain at the doorway, as an indication of privacy, and re-positioned her chair to block the entrance.

"I have lived here forever, . . . Our room is small, . . . so nothing is wasted, even space!"

She chuckled to herself at her own joking.

"Everybody here is trying to guess your name, . . . and what happened, . . . and where you come from, . . . we come from the province, but I was born here, . . . and this place is not supposed to exist, . . . So I guess I come from nowhere, . . . is it the same for you?"

Connie's conversation meandered through every topics that came to mind; the village, her interests, her likes and dislikes, struggles with people unknown who wish to dismantle her home, her family, her future, . . ."

CHAPTER 7

To the Villagers the greatest threat to their survival were the Bureaucrats and Big-Businessmen, who between them were able to harass and threaten to close down the Village whenever there was any minor infringement of by-laws; to dismantle it and disperse its population. If Shakespeare had chosen this story for one of his plays, these two `administrative bodies` of Town Hall and the Big-Business fraternity of Makarti would have been depicted as;

Two Households, both alike in dignity,

In fair Manila, where we lay our scene,

From ancient grudge break to new mutiny

Where civil blood makes civil blood unclean.

And located in-between these two `Households`, the unofficial and unspeakable `Babylon`, the `*eyesore*` of San

Juan Estero, with it`s thousand or so poor inhabitants, and top of the list for demolition and dispersal, which from time to time would be attacked by `wreckers` and `fire-raisers`, the equally unofficial means of slum clearance in Manila. These attacks on the Village occur, not only to beautify the City, but as part of occasional purges on `unofficial` homesteads as a cyclic reminder to the tax-payers and good citizens of Manila that the City politburo has absolute power and dominion over their `worthless` lives when compared to their `improvement` plans. But behind these plans is `graft`, good old-fashioned graft which oils the wheels of government and business, and which clears land for `development`, usually in the form of high-rise apartment blocks or shopping malls.

This had come to be seen as a war of attrition from both sides, and works in a wonderfully anonymous way, and because of this, the arrival of the `body` was initially seen by some of the Barangay Councillors as possibly a trick, perhaps arranged by someone in City Hall. The Villagers also assumed that `Someone`, in City Hall, who believed himself to be anonymous, was in fact well-known to the residents of Babylon, as `The Gorilla`, but whose real name was Gerald Villacorta, a dedicated Manila Public Servant who during a career of more than twenty years had risen from Postal Clerical Assistant to third Deputy of the Department of Infrastructure and Sanitation; an impressive career considering that he failed to complete his education and held no formal professional qualifications in anything whatsoever. But who was respected throughout City Hall for his adherence to Patronage and Nepotism as a means of maintaining employees' loyalty.

Villacorta had a special interest in Babylon, having one-time attempted to `court` one of the pretty ladies from that place, but he had been rejected in preference to a poor but handsome bum, an emotional wound he carried still. During most of his career at City Hall, he had been the inspiration behind the night-time attacks on the Village and other slums, and was currently nurturing a new generation of `demolishers`. He was proudly a `slogger` rather than a `thinker`, and gave preference to underlings who in one way or another resembled himself. This was not unusual in Manila`s political circles, as most of those in the top positions who had crawled to the top of the greasy pole, maintained their position by similar tactics.

And now Villacorta saw the task of demolition as requiring new-blood, and had recently recruited an eventual replacement for himself. A certain Edgar Prince Villacorta-Junior the third, the son of a distant relative living in the Province, to whom he owed an equally distant favour. The young Edgar was almost a clone of himself, holding no particular values other than a simple belief in the natural order of things and people, and now someone to be nurtured and rewarded with minor `considerations`; to Villacorta senior, mere crumbs from his banquet table.

On the same morning that Connie began her conversations with the new resident of Babylon, Edgar was re-arranging things in the postal room in the Department of Infrastructure and Sanitation, designated Room Number 1432, Corridor N, third floor, Manila City Hall. He had arrived for work earlier than usual that morning in order to enjoy the satisfaction of his new place by the window, and now strolled around the office preening himself and viewing his new desk in its privileged alcove from several angles, and imagined humbler staff approaching him and it with respect, faintly bowing and envying his position in the Department, with his view of the street.

He had promised himself that from this moment of deep satisfaction that he would record in a diary, his progress in the future through the many bureaucratic layers until the eventual time of his pension, some forty years hence. This recent achievement, had taken only thirteen months, and he had proudly informed everyone back home in the Province of his progress from the dark side of the office to the `window position`, a reward almost certainly granted for his devotion to his duties as junior postal clerical assistant, which he secretly chose to describe to himself and family as, `Deputy Information Executive`.

He gazed out of the window again along Taft Avenue and Padre Burgos Street, pityingly at the frenzied sweating crowd apparently swimming their way through the heavy traffic; as he languidly re-positioned the electric fan and re-arranged on his desk, his name-plate to best effect. A sudden thought occurred to him that a photograph of himself sitting at his new desk would complete the celebration of this event, of his first promotion, albeit minute in the grand order of the Department's history, and perhaps even less significant in the total history of City Hall, as he pondered the thought that the histories of all great institutions were composed of an accumulation of such minute events!

Life was looking up at last, he thought, for after an embarrassingly disappointing high school experience, followed by an unsuccessful (failed) college course, he considered himself fortunate that he had gained the prize of employment in City Hall, totally as a result of the good offices of a distant relative, who had somehow been owed a favour from one of the Directors, or Deputy Directors, and who it seemed bore the same surname as himself; the proud name Villacorta. But for Edgar, the addition of his middle name-`Prince`, chosen by his Lola, with the further addition of,—`Junior the third` provided good reason to believe that he was able to claim membership of a revered lineage, despite his two elder brothers dispensing with the `Junior` appendage. He basked in the thought that he, Edgar Prince Villacorta Junior, the third, had at last made the grade!

Soon the other junior clerical assistants would arrive and their work would begin, sorting the external and internal mail into small trays to deliver to the other offices in the department; the senior staff trays being of polished brown wood, with names beautifully embossed in gold leaf, and he imagine his own name there some day in the future. He had already calculated the number of steps and the time required to climb all the sixteen levels to the elevated position of Deputy Director, but unfortunately without better family connections, it would be at least twenty years, unless he could become someone's protégé, or somehow shine in his duties, then anything would be possible.

He recognised the voices along the corridor and doors opening and slamming shut, and rapidly took his seat at his desk in the contrived pose of an overseer, despite his diminutive stature and his pale plump bland face, which almost everyone immediately noticed resembled a large oval plum, dominated by his large bulging eyes. He waited but nobody opened the door; then he heard footsteps and sounds of laughter immediately outside the door, and then silence. He assumed that the other three post-room staff might be quickly preparing some small surprise to celebrate his `big-day`, but the noise drifted down the corridor and was lost in one of the other rooms.

Edgar was unaware that all of the junior clerical staff had been informed late in the afternoon of the previous day that they were all required to attend an important meeting first thing that morning. They had all been told that it was a training session, and when after waiting for half an hour for his team to arrive, Edgar went out into the corridor to check; but all was chillingly quiet and it did not occur to him that the daily routine was not as it should be, so he innocently returned to the room and watched the traffic pass by.

Meanwhile his team, as he preferred to call them, were assembled with other junior staff from all of the other departments, all together forty or so of City Hall`s foot-soldiers, and were being addressed by several very senior Administrators; their topic—Contravention of Manila's By-Laws. The meeting room had all the trappings of an austere Council Chamber, with slender Greek-style columns, and some disintegrating wood panelling around the walls, with several large chairs occupied by the Administrators, who all carried the mantle of wealth in their appearance.

Edgar`s team, Sarah, Belinda and Ricky had been among the first to arrive and had been directed to the front row of seats, and were looking over their shoulders scouring the room for their leader, and signalling to some of their buddies from other departments. They had already identified some of Administrators, but the central figure was unfamiliar to them, his appearance that of a Mao ts Tung. He stood up and looked around the room as if counting his troops, and rubbing his hands in readiness of a heavy task.

"Good morning, this is something like a training session, but as you can see there are no white boards or papers to pass around."

The Administrator swept his audience with his gaze as if checking their attention.

"You will know, or you should know that as employees of City Hall, albeit young and inexperienced, that *you* are the guardians of our lovely city . . .

That is what this address is all about . . .

The Mayors Office has called our attention to the Detractors . . .

Those who throw litter, who spit on pavements, and those who . . .

Take up residence in public places . . .

Illegal occupants . . .

Squatters !"

The Administrator peered over the top of his spectacles into the eyes of each one of the underlings, or so it seemed to them. They cringed with a mild sense of embarrassment and guilt, as if they themselves were being accused of occupying un-residential places.

"The Mayor is determined to cleanse our one-time beautiful city . . .

And he needs your assistance . . ."

At this unexpected declaration the audience started to titter among themselves, Ricky glanced sideways at the two girls, his office mates. Then the Administrator began again.

"There are too many parasites in our beautiful city, polluting and littering and squatting, and it is our responsibility . . .

We owe it to the whole population . . .

To our visitors, and future generations . . .

The Administrator stood silently starring at them, his gaze injecting his words into their souls. For a few minutes there was total silence, nobody moved, even the Administrator and his cronies seemed to be frozen, all silently motionless as if under a magic spell.

Then the Administrator extended his arms like a Christos taking bets at a cockpit and cleared his throat and made ready to speak.

"We have tried . . . Should anyone doubt it, we have tried".

The expression on his face was one of deep pain and anguish.

"And the Mayors office has tried . . .

To deal with this in a fair way . . . a proper way . . .

The Official way . . .

Now . . .

This has been thrust upon us, we have no alternative but to use alternative ways . . ."

Another calculated pause, while the Administrator again stared into his audience`s now frightened faces, and rubbing his hands again, attempting to read their reactions, which he interpreted as that of the usual and expected awe-struck obedience.

"I want you to think about this, I need not remind you that this is confidential, that we do not speak of these things to anyone outside these four walls, we are all trusted servants of our City Hall, and some of you will be invited to assist in . . . to contribute in this . . . hm . . . operation, the Directors and the Mayor look for your . . . Co-operation . . . we prefer volunteers . . .

He smiled and grimaced, and turned to the others seated behind him and mumbled something; they stood up and two security guards ceremonially opened the doors at the side of the room and the Administrators filed silently out, and after a few minutes the junior clerical staff followed them.

As Belinda, Sarah and Ricky entered the post-room, Edgar once again assumed his magisterial pose, expecting them to congratulate him instead of telling him that he had missed an important training session. Edgar's expression indicated nothing of his sudden alarm and responded as if they were tricking him, but slowly he realised that his absence might have been noticed and this bothered him, for he knew that somehow the managers knew everything that happened in that place, and that they even seemed to know what the underlings are thinking when they speak to them. He couldn't understand how they managed to do this, but assumed that their natural superiority included some kind of second sight. And he wondered then if he should find out what it is all about and if it would bring praise and kudos and perhaps promotion, for he interpreted every possibility as a step up; then suddenly it occurred to him that the morning post had not been sorted, and if there was mail for the Director, or even one of the Deputies, he would deliver it personally and show his willingness to do whatever was their bidding.

He knew the names of everyone in the Department and the exact location of each office, and eagerly sorted through the post hoping to find letters for the Director or for anyone of the Deputies, or even a manager, or a Section Head.

CHAPTER 8

Edgar, ever eager to please his masters, hurried between one office and the next, hoping to be enlightened about the project, and eventually was scrutinised by Deputy-Director Villacorta`s right-hand man, Mr. Iago Mendazo, an ex security guard (and possibly part-time Hit-Man ) with an impressive reputation in `squatter` clearance. Edgar slowly handed him the post, waiting for a sign; a tap on the shoulder or something.

"Oh, . . . you are Edgar, . . . head of our departments` postal service, . . . our Deputy Director has mentioned that you are, . . . a, . . . very keen worker,"

Iago, unaware of any literary connotations of his name, attempted to find appropriately complimentary words to soften his targets, and `good-worker`, which he realised any really impressive flourish, was the best he was able to muster in this instance.

"Yes Sir, Edgar Villacorta Sir, . . . always willing Sir, . . . for the good of the City Sir, . . ."

Edgar half-smiled, hoping to endear himself to the Deputy-Director's henchman.

"Well Edgar, as you might have heard this morning, . . . the Department has been selected, . . . Or `chosen` as the Deputy-Director says, . . . Yes chosen, . . . To get things done, . . . faster, . . . faster than `One estero at a time`, . . . our brethren in Makarti need more land, . . . primary land, . . . beautiful land, . . . land that is flowing with milk and honey, . . . as they say, . . . land without, . . . Sqatters!"

The way Mr. Iago pronounced the word squatters, with his teeth together and emphasising a kind of hissing sound, produced a visual effect of distaste.

"And Edgar, . . . to come straight to the point, we need special surveillance, and to `plant` illegal items inside one of the persistent, . . . survivors, . . . The dirty and crime-ridden `shanty` . . . item at San Juan estero, . . . you know it I suppose?"

Edgar`s eyes were blinking, partly fron excitement and partly from disbelief, disbelief at his good fortune, at his recognition, at the trust already invested in him.

"Oh Sir, . . . thankyou for your trust Sir, . . . I hope I can be of service Sir, . . ."

Mr. Iago strutted around Edgar, inspecting him, and nodding to himself appreciatively, which Edgar mistakenly interpreted as passing some identity test, as a sleuth, an undercover man, a master-spy, but in fact what really impressed Iago was Edgar`s pathetically inept appearance and stance, nobody in a million years, he was thinking, would suspect the frog-like Edgar of being a spy.

"Well Edgar, . . . what do you think, . . . it's a challenge . . . are you our man?"

Edgar swooned at these words, these sweet words.

"Oh yes Sir, . . . I am your man, one hundred percent Sir, for Manila Sir, . . . and the Deputy-Director Sir, . . . and the Mayor Sir, . . . And You Sir, . . . I was a Boy Scout when I was a kid Sir, we learned about disguises Sir, . . ."

Mr. Iago`s expression momentarily became grave, but morphed into a smile.

"No need for disguises Edgar, you need to blend in with the crowd, you have to become anonymous, a nobody, someone forgettable, . . . that is your strength Edgar, to be, . . . as the Deputy-Director has it from above, . . . imperceptible, . . . which means sort of, . . ."

Edgar was standing proudly in front of Iago, with the word `imperceptible` ringing in his ears like a clarion call to duty, it made him feel as if he was the only man capable of this special operation.

"That is all for now Edgar, . . . this is more than confidential, . . . I will brief you at some point, but for now, . . . return to your new desk, . . . and keep your mouth shut, and your ears open. We will talk later."

At this, Mr. Iago retired to the rear of the office and Edgar let himself out and hurried along back to the post-room.

CHAPTER 9

By the time Connie`s mother came to take over from her at lunch-time, she was asleep in the chair, and the patient was now lying on his side, as if he had made himself more comfortable so that he could face his companion. Ma. Theresa was surprised when she entered the small space that was his bedroom.

"I`m sorry I`m so late, . . . so many errands, and so many things to attend to, . . . but you were asleep !"

Connie stood up slowly, still half asleep and pushed the chair into the tight space between the bed and the side wall. She noticed the changed position of the body, and wedged herself back into the chair, expecting a brief chat with her Mom.

"So you are tired then my little Connie ?"

"No not really tired, . . . We were chatting, . . . and it felt as if I was letting go of something, something I was holding, . . . and it seemed to fall but it did`nt drop on the floor, . . . but I suppose I was dreaming, . . . and I heard him move, . . . and I thought some words, . . . but nothing clear, . . . but I`ve never slept like that before, . . . never in the morning, . . . but I was just talking to him as if he was awake, . . . and I thought he was talking to me, . . . but I think it must have been a sort of dream."

Ma. Theresa was waiting for more, more about the conversation.

"But he`s moved Connie, . . . look . . . he`s turned around in his sleep, . . . How could he do that, . . . how could he change his position?"

Connie was searching his body lying on its side, and his arms, now relaxed, as if he was now comfortably sleeping.

"I don`t know, but it felt as if he could hear me, and I could hear him, even though he might not have said anything, . . . as if our conversation was in a dream, . . . and he was thanking and blessing everyone, . . ."

Ma. Theresa's face showed surprise and curiosity.

"A blessing Connie, . . . really like that?"

"Not like the usual blessing, . . . silent, he was silent, sitting up in the bed, and he was silently looking down, . . . at his chest or something, . . . and gradually, . . . slowly he moved his head to look at me, and his expression meant a blessing, . . . and now I, . . . it`s as if that is when I fell asleep, . . . that he sat up before, . . . but, . . ."

Ma. Theresa embraced Connie, and wiped the signs of sleep from her face.

"Do you know Connie, . . . this is certainly a miracle, . . . its certainly not something ordinary, . . . go and get your bath now, . . . And I`ll sit here for a while, . . . until your brothers get home and then I`ll cook, . . . go and bathe, . . ."

Connie patted her Mom and went to her room.

Ma. Theresa sat in the small space beneath the tiny window, contemplating the languid body lying on its side, and hoping that she too would witness something miraculous. She was puzzled that someone who was dead could come alive again, and could stay alive without breathing and could bleed and even move, but still remain static, as if he was paralysed. But if that was true, how could he turn, and sit up and bless someone. She was more hesitant than her daughter, but she was eagerly curious.

She too began conversing with the stranger.

"I don't know how to speak to you, . . . I don`t know your language, . . . , I don`t know where you`re from, . . . but we already love you, . . . even you are not from here, . . . we love you as a brother, . . . that's right, . . . our brother or at least our relative, . . . and we want you to eat with us, . . ."

Ma. Theresa was surprised at the words she had just spoken, they seemed to have tumbled out of her mouth without much thought: so simple, and maybe even wrong, and the thought that he might not want to be listen to her, and the sudden thought that he would simply stand up and walk away. This thought stayed with her for while, as if thinking it would make it happen, and she felt impelled to correct herself, and tell him that she hoped that when he fully recovered he would stay and become part of their family.

"We are waiting for you to wake up, so that we can help you, and care for you, . . . even if we have to wait a long time, . . . we can wait, . . ."

She was having strange thoughts, thinking about how Connie had told how she had chatted, and had felt that her questions were being answered, and that this man, who was like a brother, had put words into her mouth and also into her ears. And also how impossible it would be to tell anybody, even her husband, because it really seemed as if she was not true, and making it up, like a story that was only partly true. And then a sound from him, like a word but not a word, something from another language maybe, but something like a reply, and she felt he was telling her to tell the others, so they would also welcome him as she had done.

She could hear him muttering, his lips moving but the sounds strange to her, not even like words, but she could understand everything as if in her own dialect. He spoke to her as if they knew one another, his eyes half open and scanning hers, not eye-to-eye, but focused on something beyond her, as if looking through her.

"We pulled you out of the water Sir". She said softly.

"I know ". She heard him say in a muffled voice.

"We are still worried, . . . we don`t know how you came here, . . . or who or where you are from, . . . even your name?"

She sensed his gaze shifting, his eyes focusing and his attention circling hers, his expression quizzical asking the same question.

"Visitor". She thought she heard him say.

She searched his face for signs of movement, but all was as before, like a static sculptured resting figure; yet there was an unmistakeable sensation of his presence, that he was with her and that she was under his protection, and that she could relax, and let go of her worries. She closed her eyes and drifted off as if sleeping. But the next moment she was aware of not being in the small room, but somewhere else far from the estero. Distinguishably different from a dream or a whimsical thought, or a flashback; she could feel herself there, sitting on the small chair in front of the family house in the province, with the same sounds and smells that were part of her childhood, and the two tall coconut trees by the wall, and the gentle breeze and the chickens, . . . it was all there, but she had no thoughts that this was unusual, strange or impossible, . . .

She could hear people inside the house and the sounds of washing clothes and the smells of rice cooking, and she saw herself sitting on her own small chair in front of the house, and just passing the time of day, sitting without thinking about anything, but thinking anyway, . . . about her friends and her future, and about nothing in particular, and within these thoughts she sensed, that she, as she was, was asleep, . . . sitting on her small chair, with everybody inside the house, and cat-knapping as occasionally happened in the late afternoon, when there was a sense of everything settling down at the end of the day.

The only remarkable thing about this was the sensation that she could see herself whilst at the same time being within herself, and closing her eyes and dreaming briefly of people she had known at that time but who had passed away, filing past her as she sat, sleeping and dreaming, and seeing them not in the flesh but as spectres, not walking but skipping in a strange lilting dance, swaying and half-turning to smile as they danced by to the sound of silent music. She recognised all of them, remembering and knowing them as she remembered them when she was a small girl, but most of all she recognised her diminutive lola, smiling at her in recognition that her Lola and all of her companions had `visited` her, as if to prove to her that there really is another world mostly hidden, but sometimes visible and real, to convince and comfort her.

She had known about this other world long before this event, and only discovered that there were doubts about it when she started school, and that it was something that she had to be guarded about, and even now as an adult, even secretive. And occasionally she glimpsed it when she least expected it, never when she was feeling particularly devout, but when her mind was busy on other ordinary earthly matters. Then only briefly and never directly but only out of the corner of her eye, as if its power would blind her or claim her suddenly, because she understood that no one is able to live in both worlds at the same time.

But this time it had been different, the Visitor had known her hopes and desires and taken her there so that she could refresh her memories and also that she would understand the significance of the promise of the eternal reoccurrence of events, and that this small ordinary event also had a place in his heart.

CHAPTER 10

Edgar strolled along the road by San Juan Estero alongside the strange fragile structure that was Babylon, not believing that a whole village full of people could possibly be living in this weird tunnel-like construction. Ahead of him he could see, rising out of the estero, the mountainous business towers that guard the business empires of Makarti. His mission was to reconnoitre the *eyesore* and look for possible weak-points where the flimsy citadel might be attacked or invaded, and his instructions were to be invisible, imperceptible, covert and indistinguishable from any ordinary bystander, and not to draw attention to himself in any way. He was undercover, so they said during his preparation for this operation, which he saw primarily as a means of endearing himself to his masters, with perhaps a step up the ladder towards his goal.

He walked casually along one side and then down the other side, carefully noting the number of abodes, which he assumed could be distinguished by the changes of building materials and techniques. Some sections of the flimsy village were intelligently constructed, but others were haphazard, as if blown there by the wind. He counted the number of doors and windows, and noticed after several days and nights of watching the place, that one small square window glowed in the darkness with a pale yellow light throughout the entire night. This window glowed even during a brownout, which he assumed must have been from a flashlight or something.

He watched for a whole month, sometimes disguised as a street seller or a student in a college uniform: he was convinced of his perfect `cover` but his arrival had been noticed the first day by the Babylonians, especially Connie's brothers, who left for work in Cavite very early in the morning, and returning late at night.

Edgar watched and recorded in his small notebook, their comings and goings, their shopping habits and their coupling, their children, and even recorded the colour changes in the effluence in the estero, with the occasional red discharge of menstrual blood! He observed the things they carried in and out, their meal times, and the rhythms of their daily lives, and he noted all in his small book; that it all seemed average and ordinary and similar to any other Barangay. He also noticed that there were very few visitors, in fact during his first months` observations there were none; other than a regular once a week large chauffer-driven limousine with darkened windows parked on the opposite side of the road, with occasional glimpses of a well-groomed young businessman who watched the village through binoculars from the rear window of his car. The car would wait for an hour or so late in the afternoon, and the occupant would partially lower his window and sweep one section of the village with his binoculars as his weekly routine; never to get out of the car, but stay for up to an hour and then drive off. Edgar had no way of knowing that the other predator was from the tower-block that overlooked San Juan district.

CHAPTER 11

Life in the Village was indeed as Edgar observed, for there was no reason that the presence of the Visitor should affect the daily routines of any of the families, except for Ma Theresa`s family who had taken it on themselves to keep watch by his bedside. But as far as the rest of the Babylonians were concerned the body was still there, with not much to talk about, although there had been whispers that voices had been heard coming from the small room at night, but even then nobody showed much interest after the first week of his arrival.

But one afternoon after the men of one of the lesser circumspect families had been celebrating a family event by consuming anything that contained alcohol, including an unusual recipe which contained, among other things, industrial alcohol; one of the men collapsed as if his whole body was on fire. But worse still, several hours later the man`s body was gripped by frantic convulsions and uncontrollable shrieks of pain. His poor suffering wife called one of the nurses who occupied a nearby room, but the tormented man was unapproachable, thrashing the air with his arms as if fighting a legion of devils, which in fact he was. All his petrified wife and their small children could do was to seek protection in a neighbour's room, and wait for his madness to abate. By late evening he lay on the floor, clutching his face and shouting that he could not see and that he had been blinded by the volatile cocktail. There was such a relentless commotion that several of the Barangay Councillors were called to investigate the cause of the disturbance, and were unable to agree what they could do about it. Eventually Ma Theresa joined them, and almost immediately hit on an idea! That if he could be carried or dragged to within view of the Visitor, she was sure that he would be calmed or even cured. But as there was no direct passage way to the Visitors room, the drunken man, Eddie Embudo would have be dragged and carried out of one doorway, and carried along the road and into the far-end of the Village, with access into the part where the small room was located.

Eddie was a small wiry man but immensely strong for his size, and when inebriated he was a Goliath. It was decided that the safest way to transport him was to knock him unconscious with an appropriate blow to the head, and bundle him onto an ex-government surplus first-aid stretcher, which also had restraining straps. He was quickly subdued and transported to the other end of the Village, awkwardly manoeuvred through the several opening and set-down in the passage-way outside the small-bedroom. He remained calm for a while because he was still out cold, but when he came to, and found himself tightly strapped into the stretcher, he howled like something from another world. He was screaming and cursing and sometimes choking on his own vomit, the stench of which filled the space around the small room. Ma Theresa stepped over the body and into the room and sat on the chair, and touched the open hand of the Visitor. She looked appealingly into his face and asked.

"Visitor, . . . I ask for your help and your grace . . ."

She knew that the hullabaloo from the passage-way would have alerted the Visitor, and waited for a sign that he had heard her request, but there was nothing—no indication that he was attentive or movement.

She waited and then could feel the inner calmness as before. And again the words she received were unspoken but came as a thought, which she knew were not her own thoughts, but that they needed her voice to make them believable, as if she had become the Visitor's interpreter.

"You know child, . . . nothing happens without a reason, . . . this man is in darkness of his own choice, . . . he is not of your family, . . . a lawbreaker, . . . living sinfully, . . ."

She spoke the words so that the others huddled around the stretcher in the passageway could hear her, but as the curtain had been pulled closed they could not see in, and the words they heard were as if spoken by a man.

Ma. Theresa was as startled by the words as the other listening in the passageway.

"But Visitor, . . . we are all sinners here, . . . and poor, . . . and Eddie is among the poorest, . . . and his life so tragic, . . . and not for him Visitor, . . . but for us his neighbour, . . .

and for his little wife, who he has been so abused, . . . but still loves him, . . . It is so hard for all of us, . . ."

Ma. Theresa`s own thoughts and words had come from her heart, they were the truth as she believed them, and she started to cry, not only because of her sadness but because of the harshness of the Visitors words.

"My child, . . . I know your wishes and hopes before you speak them, . . . I know also what is in your heart, . . . but you also know what is said, that those who walk in darkness will see a great light, . . . this man is too stiff-necked to see anything, . . ."

Ma. Theresa could hear the others outside in the passage mulling over this last reply, and their doubts that the Visitor could do anything to help Eddie, but they noticed that Edie had become calmer and quieter, and also appeared to be listening to the words coming from the small closed room.

"But Visitor, what must he do now, if he is blind, . . . And he becomes a bigger burden on his little wife, and his children who already sometimes cannot eat, . . . what must he do, . . . and Visitor, . . . this sinner was one of those who carried your body into our place, . . . No one is beyond redemption or beyond your help, that is what we know, . . . All of us!"

There was complete silence for a few minutes, only the sounds of breathing from those inside the passage, and the usually hubbub from the traffic outside, Ma Theresa could sense the tension of waiting in anticipation of a further rebuke, but there was nothing, no sound or movement.

"Visitor, . . . we have nothing here, . . . and all around us—our enemies are lurking like lions in the shadows, . . . and Eddie will die, . . ."

Then the Visitor spoke again, . . . forgiveness is not negotiable, . . . something to be bought and sold, . . . but is freely given to all who are repentant, . . . when he asks it will be granted, . . . because of your faith my child, . . . this man will be restored, . . . , but not yet, . . . contrition; that is his way now.

Ma. Theresa cried. She could hear sighs of relief from the others waiting in passage way, and held back the curtain.

Eddie appeared to be sleeping, and she asked the men who had carried him there to take him back to his room, and to ask his wife to bandage his eyes so that he doesn't injure himself, and to tell his wife that he will recover, all in good time, but that we are all being tested, and that she should encourage him to pray and ask for forgiveness.

Outside in the shadows on the other side of the road, Edgar was watching in the darkness, the men carrying the stretcher out of one place and back to the other end of the long tunnel-like village, puzzled by what this strange event might mean.

CHAPTER 12

On the other side of the City, in one of the tall office blocks on the periphery of Makati, Mike Borja, lounged in his swivel executive chair with his legs resting on his desk—Hollywood style, and leafed through some papers concerning his father`s current project; to accumulate as much building land within Metro Manila`s borders as possible before the expected Business—Boom raised the prices to impossible heights. His father, Caesar Borja, headed `Pinnacle`, the prize-winning Real Estate empire, and socially enjoyed the company of Senators, Judges and Senior Lawyers, Foreign Diplomats, Media Bosses, and other Celebrities, and privately joked that he is best known as the most anonymous Tycoon in Manila, which to some extent was true, for there were very few photographs published of him. He believed his invisibility was the main source of his strength; and his favourite quip,—`they can`t hit an invisible target` appeared to be correct, but in truth he was seen by many, but never identified either as a tycoon or the Manila mafia—boss-man that he was.

Mike`s position in the Company was typical of any big-Boss`s son, who it was expected one day would become the Chief, but who was currently low in the pecking-order of Negotiators; serving his time as his father constantly reminded everyone; his father believing that he would have to first prove himself if he wanted respect. And this he understood as acquiring the same panoply of contacts and sycophants, and acquiring the same negotiating skills; the means to be able to buy the same kind of favours. But for now he is responding to the same issues which brought the Clerical underlings of the Council chamber of City Hall that same month, to the business of `Cleansing` Manila, which for Mike meant clearing the slums and claiming any reclaimed land for Pinnacle Real-estate.

From his office window Mike could see the `great abomination` as the San Juan squatters village was known by the business sector, and he frequently stood by the window looking out and imagining what the view would be like if the `eyesore` were replaced by an impressive tower block of apartments, shopping mall and pleasure complex. He had been persuaded by an American investor that the Quiapo district could become the most valuable bit of real-estate in the whole of Philippines, and that he should start by clearing and acquiring land alongside San Juan Estero, which had caused him to visit the area on several occasions, to get the `feel of things`, so he told his father. But there was another less obvious reason for his clandestine visits in the late afternoon, and that was in the hope to catch another glimpse of an unusual young woman he had seen only once, but that once was enough to build a dream on, and the lady, unknown to him was an occupant of Babylon.

Being the son of one of the wealthiest men in Manila had its benefits, foremost in Mikes estimation, was access to wealthy, beautiful and interesting women. Having plenty of time and money allowed him the freedom to meet and date and dispose of the best looking girls in his social circuit, but he had become bored with their small-minded conversation about fashion and shopping, when one afternoon, through his binoculars he had caught sight of the most amazing face, the face of Connie Dela Cruz, daughter of the Barangay Captain of Babylon. This was an exceptional experience because he had been surrounded by beautiful faces all of his life and took them all very much for granted, but that fleeting sight of her face momentarily stunned him, she was different beautifully different and her face occupied his thoughts several times a day, every day since that first moment. He could see by the uniform that she was a student and calculated the-afternoon-finishing-school-time, and reasoned that eventually he would catch sight of her again, then he would speak to her and arrange a date, but recently he had spotted another student, a plump unattractive lad with bulging eyes, hanging around the same district, and constantly watching the squatters abode, and considered it possible that he might be his `beauty`s` Suitor, a thought that troubled him greatly.

And now in the office, whenever his thoughts wandered in her direction, he would move towards the window, and scan the area around the canal, hoping that somehow she would reappear and this would sustain him until the certain day when he would hold her, and possibly to become his.

He returned to his desk and called other real estate managers hoping to blot her out from his mind, at least for a while.

From what he understood of the market, the price of land had already started to increase, and the prime targets were towards the centre of Manila instead of the outskirts, and one way or another he had to acquire land in the Quiapo area, one way or another.

CHAPTER 13

The Eddie Embudo episode had alerted some of the villagers to the question of the Visitor`s identity and rumours were circulating that the half-dead-half-alive man had healing powers, and some of the women from the bottom end of the village called on Ma Theresa and asked about the progress of the man. Eddies` wife had coaxed her husband to pray for forgiveness, and their small children had spent much of their time sitting with him and fanning him with pieces of cardboard to keep him cool, and Eddie was beginning to be more attentive of his family; which as far as his immediate neighbours were concerned was near miraculous, for he was usually at the centre of disputes and disagreements, and was frequently the first one to start fights.

Ma. Theresa had expected that the Visitor would have immediately healed Eddie, and not for a moment expected him to harangue the drunken and blinded man, but when she later asked the Visitor what would happen to Eddie, he explained to her that he did not have any healing powers, and that everybody has within themselves powers to heal themselves, and the direct means to call on God for help. And she asked him also why it was possible for her to hear his words. Sometimes he answered her directly and other times he said only sufficient for her to be able work things out for herself.

"Those who have ears to hear," He said. "And those who claim to know, would not ask !"

Ma. Theresa shared the duty of sitting with him, with Connie and occasionally either of them would fall asleep whilst sitting on the chair; but they rarely found the time to discuss their separate conversations, and Connie wondered if her Mom had been able to understand some of the more serious or complicated matters which she discussed with the Visitor. With Ma Theresa it was mostly everyday domestic matters, and occasionally problems she knew about with the authorities and the usual responses from the Visitor were like words from the Gospels, which convinced her that he had been a missionary or a priest.

But with Connie, he was like a teacher, challenging and teasing her and leaving her with an enigma at the conclusion of every conversation. She sometimes found this harrowing, but as time went by she discovered that his words became like the most wonderful food which she came to cherish. He told her of the many journeys he had taken, the many beginnings and endings of events, and of places and peoples and moments, and he explained how everything contained within itself its own contradiction, that love and hate were interchangeable, and that holiness and sin were equitable in some kind of mathematical way, capable of cancelling each other out of existence, and that the invisible was not a metaphor for the material, and neither were they opposites, but conjoined like Siamese twins, and that she should spend less time with him, and more time arranging matters for the next stage of her life.

One day in a moment of what she later considered to be madness, and seeing that his appearance was beginning to remind her of the holy pictures of saints, she asked him directly if he knew who he was. His eyes opened widely and he replied enigmatically.

"Who do they think I am ?"

"My Mom thinks you are someone like Saint Anthony, Helper of the Poor; a kind of messenger or a missionary."

"And what of you, . . . who do you say I am ?"

Connie felt a cold shiver run down her spine, because she was familiar with these words and also the question, and way he had put it, at that point she knew.

"You are from God !" She said resolutely. He looked into her face with an intensity that frightened her, and which strengthened and energised her.

"You said it, . . . Talitha koum ". (Which means `little girl, get up!) "All I say and tell you has been said before, and will be repeated many times, and for each and every generation throughout the world, . . . until the end time, . . . this you will know. But while still young, you know already that I have been close to drowning, and lived among the poor and destitute and those rejected, . . . those imprisoned, . . . and I have stood with men on battle-fields and watched the carnage and suffering, . . . and stood with those before their execution, . . . I too have been wrongly accused, and yet worn the robes of honour and supped with kings and carried great burdens, . . . what glory has been accorded me even though my death and denial has been plotted more than once . . . and will be for evermore, for all of these things will be repeated many times, . . . until . . ."

Connie stood up quietly, shaking with mixed emotions and with tears in her eyes, and he sat up also, without any exertion, as if lifted by invisible hands and looking into her eyes, he extended both of his hands to her, no longer bandaged but healed with new skin, as if to receive hers as a daughter and to embrace her. She reached out to touch him, and he took her hands in his, and said.

"Little Serenissima—I call you this, . . . mother of tomorrow, . . . your prayers brought me here, . . . to be my witness!"

"I need to understand ". She falteringly replied.

"There is a season, this you already know and understand, . . . about the time when you will know all, . . . you will see and hear all that you need for your comfort and the contentment of others, . . . this you will understand . . . this is just the beginning, not even yet becoming, but before I go you will arrive, . . . go and read the psalms ! ".

She repeated these last words to herself, trying to unravel their meaning, and wondered if she should ask again, and although she heard everything clearly, his words appeared to weaken him as if his words were his energy, which had passed from him into her body; he let go of her hands, sighed and lay back on his pillow and closed his eyes as if sleeping.

CHAPTER 14

Connie`s two brothers were too involved with their prospective girl friends to spend time at home, and so came home late most of the time; too late to eat and went immediately to bed and out again in the morning before the others got up, but once in a while, some Sundays they would come home and take Connie to the shopping Mall for a treat. Over several days and nights they had noticed movements in the street outside, and seeing both the short observer and the limousine with the snooper with binoculars and assumed that they were investigators of some sort, and probably working for the government, so they tried their best to avoid them. But one Sunday they planned a party so that Connie would meet her prospective sisters-in law, at Robinson`s Mall

"Wear something special Sis, we want to make a good impression." Peter said.

"Yes we want to show you off, . . . if our ladies see how beautiful and elegant you are, they will really want to be part of our family. “Her younger brother added. Connie explained that true beauty lies beneath the skin, and if their fiancés are that easily persuaded by outward appearances, then their love was only skin deep also. The two brothers were frequently puzzled by what they thought was an old-fashioned attitude.

“But Sis, its not wrong to want to look pretty is it ?”

Connie quickly turned on them.

“There is nothing wrong in making the best of yourself, . . . that’s not my point, but just look at the girls here who fall for any gwapo guy, . . . what happens to them, . . . they get pregnant and the guys disappear, . . .”

“Only some !” Peter said, knowing that his young sister had made her point.

Yet despite her admonitions, Connie put on her best clothes, and wore her hair in a bun, and her brothers dressed as if they were already going to a wedding.

Peter decided that instead of the usual pedicab they would go by taxi, which alerted their constant observer, who immediately recorded the number-plate and appearance of the taxi-driver. At Robinsons the two fiancés were waiting for them just inside the main entrance, and warmly greeted Connie with a sisterly hug. They walked slowly around, window shopping and chatting about `likes and dislikes`, and their families and plans for the future, and finally ended up in the food court, with the choice of over twenty different food counters, each with its own `speciality`.

During the week Connie had only sufficient money to buy a cheap snack and enjoyed, to her way of thinking, the luxury of choice, and loved the rich smells of so many recipes intermingling side by side in one place. Sometimes she would spot school friends out with their families, probably eating out for a special treat, and now she was able to choose anything that took her fancy.

She waited first for the two girls to make their selection of Bangus, and then she chose the same, while her brothers ordered sizzling beef-steak, which was their usual choice. The two fiancés, Roseand Angie were from distant provinces and employees in a factory in the `economic zone`-Cavite, and had made special arrangements to get this free-day by swapping shifts with their work-mates. They were both attractive and lively women, nothing like she had feared they might be, but pretty and considerate, and hard-working, so that they were able to support their brothers and sisters through their education.

They all joked about their times together, and how hard it was working in a factory with its strict rules and how they survived them, and about their families and brothers and sisters, and finally about Connie's future. Rose, Peter`s girl asked.

"So what will you do then Sis, are you going to get some work, or finish your, . . . studies ?"

"Its hard now for my parents, . . . Always finding money for school, . . . if we were rich it would`nt matter, but its already enough if I cant continue, . . . and go to college."

The two girls and her brothers listened quietly, even though Connie was much younger than any of them they listened as if what she had to say would be serious.

"I just want to be like my parents, . . . even if that sounds sad, . . . but they are always busy helping somebody, even its not really their responsibility, . . . and that's why they will live a long time, . . . because people need them, . . . and I think God knows that, . . ."

Angie had been listening attentively and watching Connie`s expression and admiring the way she spoke so confidentially for someone still at school.

"But Sis, . . . you`re smart, . . . and elegant, . . . you could be something big, . . . A model or a business woman even, . . . then you`re family, and you`re Mom could move outa Babylon, and get a nice house somewhere, . . . would`nt you like that ?"

Connie had`nt wanted to get into this big debate so soon, and did`nt want to give the impression of patronising them, as she knew this might be what they would think; she hesitated, and then Paul intervened on her behalf.

"She`s always considering her options, . . . are`nt you sis, . . . and whatever she does, . . . it`ll be ok, . . . huh Sis ?"

The two ladies looked admiringly at her.

"But, . . . you`re so pretty, . . . don`t you have a boyfriend ?" Rose asked.

"No one asked me yet". She replied, half smiling to herself, fully knowing that she carefully avoided situations where somebody might corner her and ask her out.

"But Rose and Angie, . . . this isn't all about me, . . . I`m really happy for both you, . . . cos my brods, . . . they are good guys, . . . always working hard, . . . never mean, . . . and gwapo, . . . both of them, . . . you`re all lucky to find what you want, . . . but I don`t even know what I want yet."

They chatted happily and finished their meal, and then cruised around the shopping mall, alongside all the other Sunday afternoon families who went for the simple pleasure of window-shopping, and maybe get a MacDoes, and just chill-out, as if by looking they were able to purchase all the things they have seen and wanted.

The simple pleasures of the afternoon were soon forgotten when Connie arrived home. During that afternoon one of the villages teenage girls had tried to abort her pregnancy with pills she had bought from a market-seller beside Quiapo church, and was bleeding, drenched in sweat and writhing in agony. Her mother, who had been aware of what had happened with Eddie Embudo, in her desperation, carried her daughter to the Visitor`s passageway, believing that this had already become the way of fixing things. The teenage girl was small and waif-like and was trembling with pain and fear, one of the nurses was with her trying to stanch the bleeding.

Connie had no idea how to assess the condition of the girl, but she sensed that it might already be life-threatening, and spoke to the nurse, who explained that she needed proper medical care, and besides the family having no money there was also the problem of the girl illegally attempting to abort the foetus. She immediately went into the small bedroom, and blurted out her thoughts.

"Visitor, . . . Please, . . . we can`t let this girl die, tell me what we must do ?"

The visitor was propped-up in a half-sitting position, and seemed more awake than usual. Her looked into Connies face, his expression comforting rather than confronting.

"Serenissima, . . . this little one is one of thousands, . . . Whatever you would do, for this girl, you do it for your Father in heaven, and will be done."

He said no more. Connie momentarily put her hands together as if in prayer, and went out to the girl whose eyes were now closed in agony, her breathing heavy. Her mother was holding her hand and praying and sobbing, while the nurse was trying to cool the fever by holding a wet cloth to her head. Connie asked each of them to hold her hands, and kneeling, and holding the head of the girl, she said.

"We ask you Father to Bless this child of Yours, . . . Amen"

Connie and the other two continued to kneel and waited and watched the girl stir and catch her breath in response, and relax. The nurse removed the blood-soaked towel from the girl`s body, and washed her again. The bleeding had stopped.

"Thank God for that," The nurse said matter-of-factly. Either that was a coincidence or a miracle, . . . what do you think Connie ?"

Connies was surprised at the casual words.

"That's true of everything isn't it, . . . either everything is a coincidence or, . . . everything is a miracle, . . . but what is more important is that she is better now."

The girl was sleeping, the pain gone from her face, and the nurse wrapped a clean towel around the girl`s body, and drew a blanket over her. The girls mother whispered a `thankyou` in Connies direction, and Connie went back into the small room and sat in her usual place.

She sat quietly contemplating what had occurred and even her reply to the nurse, knowing that those thoughts had not been her own.

"Visitor ". She said. "Is this why you came here ?"

"Serenissima, . . . it is all of a piece, . . . the whole of creation is like a garment without a seam, . . . where nothing can be added and nothing taken away, . . . this is why I have come".

"But why here, to this broken and corrupted place ?"

"Serenissima, . . . you are too fast, . . . all will be revealed in time, . . . the world is like the body of man, full of pain and sadness and with oceans of tears, . . . and to this place because of your simple faith and because the poor people here live so lightly upon the earth, . . . this is the heart of the world, . . . of course there is wickedness here, why else would I come?"

CHAPTER 15

Edgar had been called into the Deputy Directors office to report on his observations; he had been told earlier by telephone that some of his colleagues had also surveyed other slums and that this would lead to a final operation which would clear all of the `cockroaches` habitats in one grand operation. It sounded to him like an action movie which hopefully would end with promotion of some sort. He trembled with anticipation.

"Come in Edgar", Mr Iago Mendozo welcomed him with an enthusiastic but caustic smile, and a swift flourish of his hand, as if sweeping him into the room.

The Deputy-Directors Office seemed strangely overcrowded with what appeared to be a platoon of noisy off-duty military men all wearing identical T shirts and all lounging casually as if they had taken-over the office for their merienda ! Edgar looked frantically for somewhere to sit, and was quickly directed by Mr Iago to sit by his side, in front of the large desk in the centre of the office.

"Relax Edgar !" Mr Iago said quietly. "This is our team of Technicians who specialise in dismantling illegal constructions, . . . experts, . . . everyone of them ".

The demolition squad raised their beer-cans in unison in Edgars direction as salutation.

Edgar beamed with smile of satisfaction. "Good afternoon Sirs." Doing his best to sound authoritative.

Mr Iago waved a copy of Edgars report in the air to grab their attention.

"We have read your observations Edgar, . . . and I should add, . . . the Deputy Director was most impressed with, . . . and our team here would like to, . . . clarify a few items, and by the way, . . . to keep you in the picture."

The toughest of the technicians caught Edgar`s eye by raising his beer can and squinting in his direction, as though catching him in his sights, for he had the mark of a military man.

"Edgaaar, . . ." He pronounced his name slowly and with emphasis.

"We have reconnoitred your patch and found it exactly as described, . . . but we are not sure about this window that glows the all-night . . . is it a kind of signalling device? . . . were there any signs of internal activity, . . . noise or voices, or other signs of activity?

His voice had a sharpness which suddenly alerted Edgar to its seriousness, for he had not expected anyone raising questions about anything, for as far as he was concerned this squatters patch was comparatively quiet compared to some of the other slum compounds.

"No, not really anything, no noises or activity, just this dim yellowish glow coming from the small window, . . . it's the only place where there is any light, . . . even during the day it`s on, . . . and at night, . . . a few students getting home after midnight, but nothing at all between two and four in the morning; everyone sleeps, . . . total silence."

"And what about on a full-moon, . . . anything, . . . anything in the water ?"

"Stillness, . . . only quietness Sir, . . . except for the sound of flapping plastic sheeting when the breeze catches the place, and the canal-water so thick with litter and things, that nothing moves in it."

"So everyone sleeps then, . . . No movement at all ?"

"Yes!" Edgar replied, . . . nothing moves at all, . . . just as if we`re in the Province".

"That`s good then, . . . so, . . . on my calculation, . . . we would have at least three hours to clear them out without anybody stirring?"

This last comment alarmed Edgar, as though he had only just, at that moment, suddenly realised how serious it sounded, and that soon all the squatters would be cleared away partly as a consequence of his efforts. Mr Iago tapped the desktop with his fingers and seemed lost in deeper thoughts.

"Will you need me anymore Sir?." Edgar asked, his eyes blinking rapidly.

Mr Iago exchanged glances with the squad commander who stealthily communicated something with his men.

"No Edgar, that`s fine, . . . we`ve got it now, . . . and thanks for your good work. It`s best for you to keep clear of that place now, . . . you`ve done your bit, . . . Now it`s our turn to do ours."

Mr Iago nodded in agreement, and standing up, signalled to Edgar that the meeting was over.

Edgar quietly edged his way through the T-shirted gang and returned to the Post Room, wondering when and how the Technicians would do their job. He knew, what was common knowledge, that slum clearance was rarely executed as described on the TV or radio news, and that it always involved force and threats and aggression, and that it was always a case of the rich against the poor, and the strong against the weak, and for him now, as an employee of City Hall, right against wrong. But that was part of his job now and part of his future, and there was no room for sentimentality or pity, and he rapidly switched his thoughts to a vision of San Juan Estero without the straggling eyesore that was Babylon, to a cleaner place without the flimsy serpentine monstrosity housing a tribe of law-breakers and tax-dodgers and `chancers`.

He whiled away the rest of the afternoon writing his `journal`; his mind wandering in and around the vicinity of San Juan, with its polluted canal and its weird assortment of apartments strung together like a long ramshackle necklace. Outside the traffic screamed and roared as commuters rushed from one Jeepney to another, and standing by the window he caught a brief glimpse of one particular figure, a slickly dressed man crossing the street heading in the direction of City Hall. The figure stood out like a sore thumb in the heaving crowd; one immaculate suited and well-groomed man striding like a conqueror. The sighting was brief but Edgar knew instantly that he has seen him several times before, . . . sitting in his car and watching the inhabitants of Babylon through his binoculars.

CHAPTER 16

The Barangay Captain casually mentioned to his wife one morning that he felt uneasy about an apparent `quietness` around the village, and began reminiscing about `old times`.

"Yes wife, in the forest we knew when there was as typhoon on its way, . . . everything stopped moving, and there was a cold silence which settled on everything, . . . then we knew something was on it`s way, . . . you never forget that feeling, . . . and it`s here now, . . . I can feel it."

Ma. Theresa had also felt something, but for different reasons, but she pretended that everything was alright; knowing that if she concurred with her husband that he would become more alarmed and start imagining the worst.

"It`s no quieter than usual." She said.

“You always like to meet trouble half-way husband, . . . and if there was something happening, someone would know, . . . I`ll ask at the market later.”

“And I`ll ask the Councillors to keep their eyes open, . . . but you`re probably right Ma, . . . I`m always expecting something to happen, and sometimes it does and sometimes it does`nt, . . . what does that say about me wife, ?”

Ma. Theresa`s thoughts were momentarily elsewhere but she replied automatically.

“It says husband, . . . you`re a good man and a responsible one, that`s what it says”.

She cleared the plates from the small table and busied herself around the tiny cooking area while her husband let himself out into the road. He walked along the length of the village, checking for anything unusual, but all seemed to be in order, nothing broken and just the usual thick grey rubbery layer of rotting paper and saturated litter stifling the stagnant canal water.

Yet the Barangay Captain was still gripped by feelings of dread, for besides his thoughts about the stillness in the vicinity of San Juan district as a bad omen, there were rumblings about the Stranger. Two of the Councillors had hinted to him on separate occasions that there was tsismis going round that the `stranger` was a fraud and a trickster, and that he would bring bad luck on the Village, and that some of the Villagers wanted him to leave. He could also sense as he walked around the Village that there were hostile feelings implicating him in protecting the wounded man, because some of events which also included his wife and daughter, the gossip included suggestions of `incorrect relationships`.

He felt trapped by the Tsismis because he was unsure how far it had reached, and tried to work out if his wife and family were aware of them. Whenever possible he avoided family conflicts, but he also knew that to hold the Villagers together against external threats, he needed their trust and respect, even from those who were troublesome or who held grudges. As for the `stranger`, he saw him as just one small problem among many others, that would eventually resolve itself, to be replaced by other, as yet unknown, priding himself in the simple philosophy of `live and let live`.

The solution, he pondered, would come of its own accord, and in the mean-time, he would continue to listen to the tsismis and keep his own counsel and wait for signs from his wife that at some point in time, they would stand together to share their problems, whatever the case.

Meanwhile Connie and her Mom continued to share their company with the Visitor unaware of the tsismis.

CHAPTER 17

Edgar expected, each morning as he arrived at City Hall, to hear of the raid and the slum clearance, and after nearly a month without anything happening, he assumed that it must have been cancelled. But since his last interview in the Deputy Directors office with Mr Iago and the Technicians, he had become apprehensive and worried about his involvement in the project. Whenever he thought about the men in T shirts he imagined them physically dismantling the village, by tearing it's flimsy sides off and exposing its inner nakedness, and the squatters huddling together like frightened defenceless cockroaches awaiting eradication; the word eradication somehow articulated itself in his vocal chords as if the word itself had hidden powers of persuasion.

He attended to his daily duties in the postal room, but kept himself more to himself than usual. There were no signs of anything happening and the daily routine continued as if the `clearance project` had been an organisation exercise, and perhaps nothing more. But one evening before finishing for the day he caught a glimpse of one the `technicians` in the compound behind City Hall, wearing camouflage cargo pants and holding military-looking packs which soldiers always carried on manoeuvres.

That evening passed but he could not sleep, imagining the silence surrounding the canal being shattered by some terrible military raid, and although it was already past midnight he decided that this must be a kind of premonition, and that he should to go to the Village and perhaps warn them, if he could find the courage.

He approached San Juan in the darkness from behind Quiapo square, and he could see that the street alongside the estero had been cordoned off with a kind of scaffold barrier, and guarded by several uniformed police and several of the T shirted technicians. There were no street lights but he knew the vicinity well enough to take a side-street to get to the other end of the village; but as he turned the corner of the street, there again was a barrier at the far end, with guards stopping night-time stragglers, and among them the elegant businessman with the binoculars.

Edgar knew that his presence would not be welcomed if not very dangerous, and that if he was seen by any of them that he might come under suspicion; but he knew the perfect hiding place where he could observe the raid unseen.

Apart from the dull yellow glow from the small window overlooking the canal side of the village, there was no moonlight and almost complete darkness, but Edgar could make-out what looked like faint shadows of activity on the grey surface of the canal, with occasional small splashing sounds. Edgar strained his eyes further to see, but he could only surmise that something was happening in the dank water beneath the village; then suddenly a loud explosion which shattered the silence, and with angry yellow flames shooting out from beneath the long tunnel-like structure. Almost instantly the village was on fire, quickly filling the air with putrid smoke. Some of the bamboo piles had been broken by the explosives and the flimsy structure was breaking apart in places and leaning over, torn like the skin of a captured serpent, revealing her innards. There were screams and shouting from inside, while the men on the outside fired their small arms into the wounded village to add to the chaos, which had all occurred in less than a minute. The frightened villagers were trapped like real cockroaches, and nothing could now prevent them from extermination by bullets or fire. Edgar was paralysed with fear, as he tried to make sense of it, watching helplessly as some of the villagers tried to escape the flames; he could see and hear the panic in their faces and their cries.

Then suddenly a louder deafening cracking sound followed by the booming tremor of an earthquake changed everything. Almost immediately this was followed by an unbelievable and instantaneous deluge of rain, like the sudden concentrated down-pour of a typhoon, as if a whole river had been poured on the village from the skies, immediately dousing the several fires which had caught on at intervals along the length of the injured writhing serpent-like structure. And then another earth-heaving jolt of another after-shock and the panicking attackers surrounding the slum-village shouting orders and attempting to save themselves and each other in the darkness.

Edgar`s thoughts were racing, as he watched the raiders struggling in the deluge to dismantle the barrier and remove themselves from the scene; they had obviously cut the electricity supply or it had been broken in the earth-quake, but now there were flashlights sweeping across the canal from inside the village, some of the attackers where in the water splashing and shouting, attempting to defend themselves from the torrential downpour.

Edgar had been hiding behind a bill-board in a part-demolished doorway of a redundant warehouse out of sight of the attackers, hypnotised and traumatised by the series of rapid events, hardly believing what had happened. Some small lights began to glow, powered by a portable generator, creating tiny rainbows in the cascading downpour. He began talking to himself, telling himself that what he had witnessed was impossible, so perfectly timed that it must have been a miracle and definitely no coincidence, and perhaps his presence had also been part of that same miracle, and that if any blame had been attached to him, then surely this was his forgiveness? But he had merely witnessed it and done nothing to help.

He ran along the road by the side of the village, shouting and waving his arms in the air, trying to engage anyone who might be looking in his direction. The village had sprung back life; there were now lights and bodies moving on the torn roof, pulling and tying and fixing polythene sheets and other scraps of metal and timber sheeting repairing the damage, and he could hear the determined voices energising their activities, and he shouted encouragement and offered assistance, but their self-sufficiency was total.

He was soaked to his skin and shivering with cold and exhaustion and began walking slowly back to his lodgings in Sampaloc; it was still too early for the dawn as he trudged past Quiapo church. And the streets were still empty as he made his way home along Espana Boulevard, still talking to himself about the miracle.

CHAPTER 18

As dawn broke the village glistened in the early sunlight as if nothing had happened; it was still raining but with no more force than a shower. Inside the Village there was the usual early morning activity as families prepared breakfast and got ready for work and school, but with more than the usual hubbub and chatter. The Baranguy Captain walked the length of the village checking that everybody was alive and well, and was welcomed with exultant hugs, handshakes and congratulations as if he had personally brought them through the night of terror. Almost all of the damage had already been fixed, and there was general agreement that City Hall had been behind the attack, but some voiced opinions that the raid had been brought on by the presence of the stranger in their midst, while others suggested that it had been `He` who had caused the earthquake and the deluge, that had been their salvation. The Barangay Captain agreed that `good always followed bad` and that tsismis was always jumping to the wrong conclusions.

Ma. Theresa and Connie called in at the Visitor's small room to check that he had survived the attack. Together they asked him if He had caused the earthquake, but as usual there was silence. After the brief questions, Ma Theresa left Connie alone in the small room. Connie closed the curtain behind her and drew her chair out of its corner, and sat as had become her habit

"They are all talking about our miracle." She said quietly, waiting for a reply, . . . then the slightest movement of his lips.

"Serenissima." He said, his voice again sounding in her head.

"Little one, . . . there is no miracle ! . . . such things belong in the minds of men, . . . they need such simple beliefs for their comfort and their understanding, . . . but you little one must not think that way, . . . what you witnessed was an ordinary token of love and such things happen everyday."

Connie felt frightened by the strangeness of the words and solemnity of the sounds as she heard them, and had hoped to hear something uplifting and triumphant, and about survival of the village and hopefully of God`s grace. But she was held by the usual feeling that there was never quite enough to help her make sense his words.

"Sir, . . . so was it a coincidence then, . . . is it possible that this happened without God`s blessing?"

"Serenissima, . . . be calm, . . . I know your doubts, . . . but you know it is written that not even the smallest bird shall fall from the sky without your Father`s knowledge, . . . all that you know is of this world, of the world of men . . . but the time will come, . . . when you will know, . . . I have many things to tell you, . . . that is my purpose here, . . . but for the present time, . . . be still."

Connie felt overwhelmed by her thoughts as usual, as she tried to unravel what she knew to be beyond her understanding, and she felt unsettled as if these conversations had become like a game, intended to confuse her. She sat silently, wondering how she could find the words to express her thoughts and feelings. She could hear excited voices outside in the street, and presumed that there her neighbours were celebrating. She went to the family room to look out and saw the small crowd of strangers gathered in the road, with her mom and dad talking with police and what looked like reporters and camera-men, and there were also limousines with officials and business people, as if the Village had become the focus of public attention. She waited for the show to finish before she went outside into the street, into the street of men.

She stood for a while as an outsider, at the edge of the gathering, listening to the interviews and the many `eye-witness` accounts of the miracle, the act of god, the blessings of Santo Niño, the fortunate coincidence, and the freak storm. She wanted to become invisible to witness. Passers-by stopped and joined in the discussions, swelling the crowd further until it completely blocked the street. She heard her dad denying that anything of importance had happened, and that the noises had been from fireworks, not bombs or demolition devices. She quickly realised how he had intended to play it, and this too she saw as a token of love.

Some of the Villagers told their own versions of the event, and the various reporters collected between them their stories as parts of a rich tapestry of Quiapo life. The photographers and the cameramen recorded faces, but when they looked around for signs of the deluge and the fires and the damage, there was nothing to shoot. Like all public gatherings this one followed its laws of sudden and rapid expansion and slow dissipation, and before merienda time it had dissolved completely.

CHAPTER 19

Edgar went to work without any sleep, uncertain what the day would bring. He followed his usual daily routine whilst keeping an eye on the amount of traffic in the corridors, but all was as usual. He decided that it would be safer to hand out the important deliveries to his team and keep a low profile in case of any backlash, but none came, and he managed to stay awake until the end of the day. But it had been a day of soul-searching, and he had been troubled by mixed feelings of whether he could carry any of the blame, especially as he had been under orders. And up to that point he had seen his role as a mere `foot-soldier` carrying no legal or moral responsibility for his asctions, somehow in his mind the bosses would shoulder all blame, but now questions came at him from all directions. What if he had been asked to plant a bomb, or in former times to have been one of José Rizal`s execution squad, could he have done it, and would he have fired the shot that killed his nation's hero ?

His troubled thoughts were punishing him; little lies and small deceits were part of everyday life, and he was no different from anyone else. When he heard or read about corrupt governments, and senators and judges, and city mayors, and policemen, and even humble traffic cops, it was because graft and corruption was normal. He asked himself how it could be otherwise; their slogan was that power corrupts, and that corruption equals power which fans out in one way or anther as the route to a desirable life-style. How could it be otherwise?

But now there were bigger issues, he had witnessed a miracle and perhaps even been part of that miracle as the only observer, but because of the corruption he could not reveal it, or tell it to anyone, unless he became anonymous. But where was the moral responsibility in that?

He could`nt leave his job: that would change nothing, for there was nowhere to go, no corruption-free zone in Manila, or even wider afield, even all the way back to his Province. He felt trapped by his new realisation!

CHAPTER 20

Caesar Borja had spent the whole morning on the telephone, talking to City Hall, and to the Senators who had already invested money in the intended development projects, and the Mayor, his lawyers, and finally to Mike, his son.

"I thought this was all ready to roll !" He shouted down the phone.

Mike Borja had also been heavily engaged in phone calls, mainly to Mr Iago Mendozo, enquiring why the clearance had failed.

"Did`nt you hear the news?" Mr Iago asked.

"What news? I`m not interested in news, . . . you chose the team, you took the cash, . . . you agreed the deal, . . . and now I have half of Manila wanting to kick my butt."

There was silence for a few minutes, as Mr Iago searched the appropriate words to explain.

"It went according to plan, . . . exactly to plan, . . . then outa nowhere one Christ-almighty quake and rogue storm, . . . it was on the news, . . ."

"I don`t listen to the news, I rely on facts and deals, and now, . . . you have failed, . . . and the Company has a massive problem."

"But Sir, even the Press is calling it an act of God, . . . we can`t, . . . dare not go back there for a while, . . . we could use some of the other options, . . . but nothing secret . . ."

Mr Iago had intended mentioning returning the money paid for organising the raid, when Mike Borja slammed the telephone down in his frustration and anger.

CHAPTER 21

By mid October the man they called `Visitor` exclaimed that he would end his forty-day fast, and that he was hungered; and was asking for bread.

His voice was soft like that of a weary traveller, and when he spoke he moved his hands as if in supplication.

"Rice!" Ma. Theresa said. "There is no bread here, but rice only."

"That is sufficient, . . . whatever your family eats I also will eat, and whatever they drink, that also shall I drink, for here we are all one flesh."

His words had the rhythms of the Psalms, as if they were part of his remembered vocabulary. Ma. Theresa did not understand how this could be possible, how He and her family could be of the same flesh, but she smiled with satisfaction at the thought of it. She could see that he was now stronger and steadier in his movements, and that his voice was no longer in her head. He was sitting up looking at his hands.

"Visitor, I will prepare you food, and bring you some clothes if you are feeling well enough . . . we are happy that you are well now, . . . while you were recovering we bathed your body and attended to your wounds, . . . but you would not eat, and we were worried that you would become weak and become thin, and waste away."

She waited for his reply.

"Sister, . . . you know that I would not die while I am here with you, and you know also that whatever you do for me is an act of charity, . . . it is true that I was not strong, but what little strength remained I conserved because of my fast, which was required of me, . . . but all that you did is here".

He brushed his temples lightly with the fingertips of both hands, indicating that he remembered everything, and then placed his hands on his heart.

Ma Theresa had not been prepared for this sudden change in his wellbeing and was now rapidly thinking of practicalities; of how he would bathe himself, of what clothes he would wear, and how he would occupy his time, and how he would fit-in with her family and neighbours, now that he was fully alive.

"I know your thoughts Sister and I say this to you, . . . my needs are simple, . . . but you know the parable of the Good Samaritan?"

"Yes Father." Without thinking her response was automatic.

"No Sister, I know that in your heart and in your soul that you think you know who it is that I am, . . . but here, . . . I am your Brother, . . . and my daily need will not be a burden to you or your family, . . . do you not know that ?"

Ma. Theresa hurried to the market, and on her way there she called in at the church for a quick prayer of thanksgiving for the recovery of her Visitor, and to light a candle. She then searched among the roadside market-stalls for clothes for Him, without knowing what would be appropriate. For in her minds-eye, she imagined him wearing something regal and flowing, and she had also thought that somehow she would have been directed by an invisible power, but her mind was a blank and she decided to wait until she had spoken to Connie about it. But she was sure that He would enjoy the fish that she had bought, and the fresh vegetables.

When she arrived back home, she started preparing the food straight away, and went to the small room to tell the Visitor about her morning's shopping. The curtain was tied back and he stood fully-clothed in freshly washed Jeans and a black T-shirt, and looking out of the small window. She was sure that he must have heard her, but he did not turn round to greet her but remained trance-like looking out of the window.

She asked him hesitantly. "Visitor, . . . shall I tell everyone that you have recovered ?"

He slowly turned to face her, his eyes holding hers.

"Sister, . . . Please wait, . . . I am grateful for your love and care and faith, . . . but I know there are doubters here, . . . for they have their own burdens, . . . and they live in hope, . . . but they are suspicious and frightened, . . . soon they will come to know me, or come for me."

"Yes Visitor I understand."

But he could see that as she spoke a small look of doubt appeared in her eye and that she seemed agitated, and he thought that perhaps she had been searching or hoping for something more, some reassurance that would settle her mind.

"Sister I know that you are troubled about many things, . . . about my presence here, . . . and your expectations, . . . Your faith is strong because it is simple, that is no criticism and in many ways a virtue, . . . and as you say to me, . . . life is hard and full of contradictions, . . . on earth as it is in Heaven, . . . yes sister, . . . You will learn that the whole of creation is contradictory, how could it be otherwise? . . . But you have your simple faith, and hope and charity, . . . and finally everything comes down to these!"

Theresa could feel his strength enter her body like the instant taste of labuyo-chilli-vinegar on her tongue or the sudden coldness of rain on her skin, and this thought brought tears to her eyes,

"Yes Sir, I know and I try to understand, . . . and we all pray for that, . . . but Sir, . . . what of the church and the Priests, . . . are they not with you also ?"

They stood close enough to touch, but the distance she felt rise up between them, like an early morning mist in the fields chilled her, and she sensed his sudden resistance to reach out to lay his hand upon her, perhaps to bless her, noticing the slightest change of movement in his expression.

"Sister, . . . even the Churches, and they are legion, and those within them, . . . remember the story of the tares among the wheat, and how it is better to let them grow together until the harvest: and that in the time of the harvest the tares will be gathered together and bound in bundles and burnt, this is true even of the churches, . . . the tares will be separated from the wheat, and besides, . . . remember there have been money-lenders in the synagogue."

Ma Theresa was frightened by this, and could not easily find words to express her thoughts; she felt panicked by its suddenness.

"But what of us here, . . . my family, . . . Visitor, are we saved?

"Sister you should know what has been written and what has already come to pass here in this place, that I was a stranger and you took me in as if I were a little child, and clothed me and visited me and blessed me with your care, and all of this without expectation of reward, . . . you and all of your family did this in good faith, you are all are good Samaritans and are assured of eternal life."

Ma. Theresa felt her apprehension ebb away, like the lull after a strong wind has abated, and she felt a feeling of calmness come over her.

For the first time since the attack on the Village all of Ma. Theresa`s family were together, her husband and Connie and her two brothers and the Visitor sat round the small cramped table for what Ma. Theresa described as a celebratory meal. The small shack of a room was used as a family room, and contained most of their possessions, which had to be removed to other spaces to accommodate the small dinning table, which on this special occasion had been prepared unusually with a real linen table-cloth. It gave the room an elegance which pleased Ma. Theresa, especially as each of the others cooed appreciatively as they took their places. Visitor sat silently at the head of the table while Connie and her Mom brought in the bowl of steaming rice, the fried Bangus and the vegetables. This was also the first time that Ma Theresa had served food as if it had been a banquet and she could sense the unspoken pride on the faces of her family.

"Visitor, please kindly say Grace". She asked in a whisper.

The Visitor nodded to the others and held out his hands in supplication, the centres of his upturned palms displaying the dark scars of his wounds. He closed his eyes.

"Heavenly Father, Bless this food to our use and Us to Thy Service, and deliver us from evil, . . . Amen.

Connie recognising that her two brothers were both unsure of how they should address the Visitor, she introduced them and her father.

"Sir, . . . these are my two brods, Peter and Johnny, and this is my Dad, who is the Barangay Captain, . . . they are a little shy Sir because usually we do not eat in this way, . . . Because our space is small and our work is always waiting."

Her two brothers smiled in appreciation for Connie`s explanation, and the Visitor placed both hands together as if in prayer, and looked into the faces of each of them.

"I am grateful for that Serenissima, . . . I am a little hesitant also, . . . for I arrived here as a stranger, and I have become as a Son of the family, . . . this fish is delicious, . . . let us eat and enjoy."

And as they ate they lost their shyness and the careful table-manners of eating with strangers, and shared the intimacy of family-closeness and shreds of tsismis with one another. Besides Connie's few words of introduction there were no rituals which drew them together as a family, they became comfortable sitting together around the meal-table as if they had settled any doubts or questions. Peter talked about his work repairing fishing boats and Johnny chatted about his girl-friend and asked the Visitor if he would like to be his Ninong, and John, Ma. Theresa`s husband conjured up stories from his Forester`s days, and finally they asked him about his past-life.

"I am, as you know, a stranger here, and a visitor without a name, . . . but never-the-less a man you have accepted as a brother, . . . my distant memories are always of places like this, . . . simple and frugal, but places near to God, . . . with the sounds in my ears of waves lapping the shore, . . . and the smells of the wind and the earth in my nostrils.

All that I am I cannot yet share . . . only because I myself cannot yet say what brought me here, . . . but I know that I am here to be with you, . . . I am called by many names, . . . according to how I am received, . . . here . . . I am, . . . received as Visitor, . . . And for the moment this name is convenient, and describes what I am."

These were the first words that they had all heard him speak, and apart from the conversations Ma. Theresa and Connie had personally experienced, they all had heard the true sound of his voice, which was that of an orator or a teacher; his words spoken with a gentle yet unquestionable authority, but the effect and sense of what each of them had heard, they could see in each other`s faces. For John and the two brothers there was incomprehension, as if they had been stunned into silence, for Ma. Theresa there was magnanimity and humility, but for Connie there was graciousness and tenderness, and the realisation of affinity.

The Barangay Captain continued to pick at the remains of the fish with his fingers, and had been mulling over in his mind about how he might be able to help `Visitor` to recover fully.

"Visitor, my family are happy that you are stronger now, . . . and I am wondering how we can help you so that you can walk around more, . . . and even visit the town, . . . that is, if you want it?"

Visitor put his hands together again in his characteristic way while he considered his reply.

"I am already strong, . . . and able to walk among your neighbours, . . . but I am also aware there are dangers and snares here, . . . that I am not yet wise about, . . . but there will be a time, . . . and I will look to you, . . . and to your sons, . . . and walk with you by the sea . . ."

"And we can take you on a trip, . . . along the coast, . . . when you are ready !" Johnny said enthusiastically.

"Yes and fishing in the Bay if you want?" Peter added.

Ma. Theresa was pleased with the quickness and the easiness of the exchanges between the Visitor and the men in her family, but for a while she had been gazing down at the remains of the meal lost in her thoughts, and thinking ahead and speculating on how Visitor would feel about the forth-coming Christmas-time, and the January Fiesta of the Black Nazarene, especially as he still bore the wounds of the Crucified Christ. She looked up at him, caught by his gaze, as if he knew her thoughts.

"Sister, . . ." He said. "I have witnessed these things many times before, . . . they have their own meaning, . . . and opportunities, . . . to glimpse something extraordinary, . . . that is no bad thing!"

The others looked at him, baffled that he seemed to have answered an unspoken question, the same question which had just also passed through their own minds. The two brothers excused themselves and Connie helped clear the table, and offered to tidy the small room.

CHAPTER 22

There are very few secrets kept by the Babylonians, and by the time the Dela-Cruz family and the Visitor had finished their first meal together everyone in the Village knew that He had recovered and was able to enjoy the simple but important pleasure of eating Bangus. Some of the children from the other end of the Village, who had listened to the many titbits of gossip about the `dead-man` who had come back to life, pestered their elders to be taken to his small room to witness `the miracle` of his resurrection. And like most events or `happenings` in the Village which begin in a haphazard and individual kind of way, they rapidly trigger a frenzied swarming instinct among all of the inhabitants. First to call-in was the tiny girl who had initiated the whole event which led to his rescue and recovery from the canal. Her mother held her hand while the child carried a fresh Sampaguita necklace as a gift for the Visitor. They both stepped inside the entrance of the small room and waited for him to turn around from the small window.

"Sir, . . . we have come to greet you, . . . it was my daughter Sir, . . . who found you in the water Sir, . . . we are so happy you are well Sir." The mother said falteringly.

Visitor turned to face them and extended his outstretched hands as a greeting, he smiled at the child and touched her head in a kind of blessing.

"What is your child`s name ?" He asked the mother.

"Adele Sir, . . . we call her Adele, . . . but we could`nt afford the baptism yet Sir, . . . so we can change it to something else if we want, . . . Sir."

He sat on the bed so that he could more easily look into the child`s face.

"She is a beautiful child, . . . and the name suites her well, . . . bring me some water."

The woman was not sure what he had meant, and thought that he needed a drink, and called into the nearest room for a glass of water for the Visitor. When she returned her daughter was sitting on the Visitor's lap and chatting with him. She handed him the glass of water, but he did not drink, but placed it on the chair and without speaking, he dipped two fingers of his right hand into the water and made the sign of the cross on the child`s forehead, saying.

"I baptise this child, . . . In the name of the Father, . . . the Son, . . . and the Holy Ghost, . . . I name thee, . . . Adele, . . . Gabriel, . . . the bringer of Good news, . . . Amen."

And just as he had uttered the final word, they were joined by other mothers and their children who crowded around him, and filled the narrow passage way that was the main corridor through the centre of the village.

Adele`s mother knew that the brief ceremony was real, and could feel the presence of a transcendental power filling the small cramped room. She took her daughter from him and clasped the child to herself.

"Amen Sir, . . . We are happy you are with us."

She moved aside to allow others to draw close to him. Some brought flowers, and candy, and others brought rosaries for him to bless, and small bottles of water, which they had expected him to bless. And as each parent and child moved out of the small room, their places were taken by others; some came simply to see him and to greet him, others hearing that he had brought instant comfort to others came also to ask for a `Blessing`, and some told him of their failings, or their hopes and desires, or asked him to interpret their dreams, to predict the future, or to tell them the secrets of long-life.

Finally a couple, both pitifully thin, with three equally undernourished children, all of them exact copies of their mother, came in, all holding hands.

"Sir, . . . I have come to thank you and to ask forgiveness, . . . I am Eddie Embudo Sir, do you remember me, a stupid man, . . . whose life you saved, and now Sir, I come to show you, . . . how I have changed.

Still holding hands, they edged their way into the small room, their faces showing their eagerness for simple recognition and acceptance.

"Yes Eddie, . . . but you have come here so that you should know the truth, . . . it was not I who saved your life but your wife's faith, . . . it is your wife who redeemed you, . . . for you have been blessed with a loving family, . . . and for that you should be grateful, . . . but bring the children closer that I can see them."

Eddie and his wife manoeuvred the three small children into the cramped room as if they were fixed extensions of their own bodies, until they were within his reach. He extended his hand to touch each of their heads, and uttered something which they could not understand, but which both mother and father interpreted instantly as something mystical and which brought a healthy glow to the children's faces. Then he raised his hand in the sign of the cross as a blessing.

"The Peace of the Lord be with you, Louise and Eddie, and to each of your little ones."

As the little family edged their way out through the door-way of the room, their hands still locked together, Eddie's wife reminded him that she had never told him her name, and yet he had known it.

As each of his visitors returned to their own rooms, they shared their excitement with their immediate neighbours and relatives, and quickly, the power of their tsismis assumed the mantle of the power of the Holy Spirit. As each small interlude was described and repeated, the tsismis gathered momentum generating belief and hope and reverence among them; some of them declared that He was the Messiah returned to save the world, while others believed that he was probably one of the disciples, although there was no agreement on which one he might be. Their stories were woven together like the re-cycled fabric of Babylon itself, which carried them through that evening and the whole of the night and into the following day.

CHAPTER 23

As the dawn arrived, He stood motionless by the small window gazing out at the near empty street, following with His gaze the occasional pedestrians as they passed by. All of them walking purposely and hurriedly by; none of them turning their attention to look in His direction. Within the Village the day was also beginning, which was the most active time of the day, as each fragment of the community variously bathed and dressed and prepared their breakfast, and bickered and cajoled and shouted at one another. To Him there was something welcoming in this daily ritual which pulled Him back to His own childhood.

He had not noticed Connie enter the small room and stand close behind him, almost touching him, and she waited several minutes for him to turn round but he seemed transfixed on the street outside, as if he was expecting something or someone, finally she spoke.

"Pardon me Sir, . . . my mom wants to know if you would like to take a bath and have some breakfast, . . . because she has to go to the market shortly, . . . ?"

He turned away from the window, and looking into her eyes he held out his hands as if to take hers in a greeting, but as she moved towards him the greeting became a hug, and wrapping their arms around each other as if in a lovers' embrace. It had happened in a flash, instinctively and uncontrollably; she felt his breath on her face and the warmth of his body against hers, and in the heat of the moment she seemed to lose consciousness, her mind blank.

"Serenissima, . . . I can hear your heart beating, . . . do not be afraid, . . . or surprised, . . ."

For an eternity they stood holding each other without any thought of letting go.

"I`m not frightened, . . . sometimes I have had a premonition of this, . . . exactly like this, . . . but even then I did`nt expect . . ."

They dropped their arms and they sat down, he on the bed and she on the chair.

"Sir, . . . my mom has made a space for you where you can take a bathe, . . . it is`nt like a bathroom, . . . its like everything here, . . . we call it `makeshift`, . . . but you have your privacy, . . . and you also have your place at the table, . . . and there is some pandesol for your breakfast, . . . and later I will get you some more clothes, . . . And you will be able to, . . . just go where you want, . . . even along the road just outside there."

She pointed to the places outside the window, and took his hand and led him to the makeshift bathroom, a quickly constructed cubicle overhanging the canal, with a large round metal tray to stand in and a plastic bucket full of clean water. She brought him soap and a towel, and left him to himself.

After he had dressed, they sat together at the small table and ate breakfast and drank warm weak coffee.

"Sir, . . . if I knew your name it would be easier for us to talk together."

He looked slightly uncomfortable at this, as if he was searching for something to say.

"Serenissima, . . . Connie, . . . Little-One, . . . this is not easy for me, . . . and also for you it is not easy, . . . but you are right, . . . it would be easier if I had a name, . . . let me tell you, . . . even if this sounds to you strange, . . . since as far back as I can remember I have always been reaching for a name . . . you know I am who I am, . . . and I know that you will understand this, . . . whatever name anyone gives me defines their relationship with me, . . . and with themselves, . . . that is why my name is paradoxical. But you already know who I am, . . . but can you imagine what might happen if all was revealed ?"

"Yes Sir, . . . I understand all of what you have said, . . . and all of the things you have told me, . . . and sometimes

I wonder why all this is happening here, and to me, . . . because I realised some time ago that somehow I am part of whatever it is that is happening, . . . and I know that you know that I am thinking about this all the time, . . . it is like something unfolding and I know that I am part of it, . . . I do not know how or why I am involved."

With this she hoped that he would at last explain to her, as he has promised so many times.

"Serenissima, . . . have you thought why I called you this, . . . and why I could not call you by your other name, . . . it is the same for you, . . . you alone know who I am, . . . call me what you will, . . . and it is as you say, . . . you are part of this story, . . . and for the present, . . . it is easiest to call me by the name the others here in the Village know me by, . . . also a name not far from the one my parents gave me, . . . here they call me Joe!"

Connie whinced.

"So I will call you Joe then, . . . like the others, . . . it sounds so, . . . so anonymous, . . . but I shall tell them all, . . . that is your name, . . . is that OK ?"

"Serenissima,. when we are together like this, . . . what we are today comes from our thoughts of yesterday, and our present thoughts build our life of tomorrow: don`t you know our life is the creation of our minds and our hearts, . . . and the words we use become more like poetry, . . . because the meaning is not in the actual words but in the rhythm of what is said, . . . we must forget the actual meaning of the words, . . . sometimes they have no meaning, . . . you have to pay attention to the energy, . . . and to the rhythm of the silent music, and if what I say to you is obscured at first, . . . and if you are searchinh for it`s meaning as if lost in the mist, . . . wait and listen to the beat, . . . there will be a turning point, . . . then you will know, . . . for meaning always waits to reveal itself to you, . . . where ever you are"

Connie turned her head away from his gaze, as she felt the tears welling up again in her eyes, . . . she wanted him to know that she understood what he had said to her, but she also wanted him to know that she had sensed something deeper, . . . which she could not explain, . . . a connection with him and an affinity that puzzled and fascinated her, . . . her words did not come easily, but she began hesitatingly.

"Yes, . . . I know, . . . I have been trying to think about these things, . . . especially about the music of the words, . . . I could see that for myself, . . . is`nt that why the psalms and the prophecies are written like that, like poetry . . . but these sounds hypnotise me, . . . they are like dreams, . . . are we then dreamers, . . . of something more real than life, . . . ?"

His expression became that of a teacher.

That is exactly it, . . . it is only through dreams that life stays awake, . . . this dream, . . . your dream, . . . our dream is a vision of the possible, . . . the difference between a dream and spiritual reality is transcendence, . . . and . . . We, that is our Being, . . . is always becoming, . . . like the whole of creation, . . . in truth there was no simple moment of creation, . . . no past tense, . . . Our Father did not create the universe as something finished and final, as a potter turns a pot on his wheel, . . . Our Father actually became it, . . . His

Spirit becomes flesh . . . this is the truth, . . . when we say that the word becomes flesh, . . . we are speaking about the poetry of the whole of existence, . . . and about the rhythm of God`s thoughts, . . . this world of men is in too much of a hurry to wait for the meaning to reveal itself ! . . . but now, . . . you almost have it, . . . and you will come to know it more, . . . yet only when the form is clear to you will the spirit also become clear. And please remember, this place is but a tiny dot in the whole of creation, . . . but even so He watches over us."

Connie closed her eyes trying to visualise images she had seen of the hugeness of the galaxies and descriptions of the origins of the universe, and of the Big-Bang, and imagined the energy he called God, not just raw energy, but mindful energy with a Name and purpose transforming Himself into the physical world and the universe.

"So that means if everything is God, . . . He is flowing through everything, . . . but how about evil, . . . is He there also?"

He looked at her and slowly shook his head.

"Yes and no, . . . do I have to keep reminding you of contradictions, . . . that is why men on earth should never judge one another, . . . only at the final judgement, whenever that time comes, . . . will resolve everything, . . . for the moment Connie, all you need to keep in your mind is that, . . . God realises Himself through physically becoming the universe, . . . which ebbs and flows, . . . between the physical and the spiritual, . . . for what other reason would men die? . . . in death we return to Him as part of that continuous flow of creative energy, . . . how else do you think I am able return here and become as I am?"

Connie closed her eyes to counteract any of the distractions of his physical proximity; for she needed to pay attention to the stresses and pitch of his voice and to hear and grasp the rhythms, but she had been way-laid on the road of her thoughts by those eerie resonances of his voice; as sharp as gravel and as soft as the whisper of frozen breath in empty space; somehow to her the same secret alchemical combination of her favourite Soulful blues music in the songs of Bob Dylan, Eric Clapton, Dire-Straights, and others.

"You almost have it!" He said.

"Yes, nearly, . . . but my head is spinning now, . . . I need to think my way through it."

It was in the full-flow of these images and remembered moments that she now sensed a presence of something more subtle, powerful and fundamental, flowing through even the smallest every-day rhythms of her ordinary daily life, as she unravelled her thoughts.

It had seemed to Connie that they had been chatting for only a short time, but her mom returned from the market laden with bags of shopping, and had heard them talking, and had been unsure about interrupting what sounded like serious discussion. She stood outside the eating-room and waited a while, but finally she stood at the entrance.

"It`s already afternoon Connie, and I need to prepare the dinner, . . ."

Ma. Theresa greeted Visitor with a smile of gentle satisfaction.

"Visitor, . . . when you feel ready, . . . we can take you into town, . . . its nice to take a walk, . . . the weather is fine and you can experience Quiapo, . . . and even visit the church if you want to, . . . ?"

"Mom, . . ." Connie interrupted her mom`s enquiry, and whispered close to her ear.

"I suppose he already knows that some of the families here call him Joe, . . . and He likes it better than Visitor, . . . so, . . . from now on it`s Joe, . . . even if it does sound a bit anonymous."

Joe had guessed what Connie was saying to her mom and raised his eye-brows Pinoy-style in acknowledgment.

Ma. Theresa warmed to this new familiarity, and ushered both of them out of the cramped room as another invasion of children and mothers could be heard congregating in the narrow passage along the side of Joe's small cell-like room.

CHAPTER 24

Connie accompanied Joe to greet the visiting mothers and their children, who rushed to touch him and embrace him. Connie was immediately concerned by this swarming assembly for she knew already that some of the mothers had recently been involved in petty criminal activities and her thoughts were that they might in some way exploit Joe, because almost certainly he would not understand their world of scams and fixes.

Joe moved his hands above his head in a sign of quietening them, and asked them if there was somewhere with more space where they could gather and sit and talk together.

"Yes Sir." One of the mothers shouted from the back.

"At the far end of the Village, . . . at it`s tail, . . . there is the place where we will sit, . . . and we can have our meeting, . . . do you want to go there? . . ."

The others answered for him, and even the little children concurred, for it seemed that they had already discussed this and agreed among themselves. Connie and Joe followed them through the narrow rickety passage-way that was the spine of the serpentine structure, passing through the segments which were the various family spaces, all of them approximations of the idea of houses lining a narrow road, but here miniaturised and strung together to form the amazing bridge-like structure suspended above the canal.

As they passed through, Joe touched with his finger-tips the fragile surfaces which divided one dwelling from another, and marvelled that such flimsy walls were capable of containing families, sometimes with as many as six or more children, and as they passed the open doorways, he saw their orderliness and neatness and cleanliness; here was frugality and dignity and homeliness, and yet here also was a dispossessed people making the most of what little they owned. Finally they reached the common space at the serpent's tail, a space that had the appearance of a covered veranda or the aft-end of a river pleasure-steamer. The children immediately squatted on the floor and their mothers leaned or sat where-ever there was something which resembled a sitting place. One of the mothers brought Joe a chair, and Connie stood by his side.

"I am pleased to see you again." He said.

"And also you, . . ." They all replied.

One of the mothers who Joe recognised as one who had come to see him previously drew his attention by raising her hand.

"Sir we are so delighted you are risen, . . ."

Some of the mothers and children chuckled at this, but she continued.

"We know you are special Sir, . . . and how you saved our place from the storm, and how you healed and helped some of our sisters and brods, . . . and we are grateful for your blessings sir, . . . which we know will help us, . . . But Sir, . . . we also want to know if you can assist us in our poverty? . . . Here in Quiapo, . . . it gets harder Sir, . . . that is why sometimes we steal, . . . and commit sins Sir, . . . how can we live without help?"

The other mothers nodded in silent agreement and waited for his reply.

He put his hands together as if about to pray, and raised his eyes above them as if looking somewhere far away.

"Sisters, . . . and little ones, . . . our Father knows your needs, . . . and intercedes more often than you realise, . . . even in the smallest matters, . . . and you know already that you—the poor will inherit the earth, . . . , and that finally, . . . the first will come last, . . . and the last, . . . first . . ."

The woman interrupted him.

"But Sir, . . . What about now ? . . . Our children cannot wait until the end of time, . . . for the time of final judgement, . . . Our trial is now Sir, . . . when we have no food Sir, . . . and we are praying, and thinking who can we ask, . . . and those we ask are also poor, . . . what can they do? . . . and our children Sir, . . . they become hungry and sick, . . . and we have no money for medicine, . . . and some die, . . . is that also our Father`s will ?"

Connie`s immediate instinct was to protect Joe, and to intervene and divert what she saw as an unfair attack, but he moved his hand in a calming motion.

"You are right to ask this, . . . and I understand what you are saying to me, . . . but you know that your Father in heaven is not like a magician, making food appear suddenly where there was none, . . . I tell you this, . . . seek, . . . and you will find, . . . I promise you this, . . . where you see His Holy Name, . . . knock and it will be open to you, . . . and those things that you do when you are desperate, . . . as you say, . . . breaking the Holy Commandments, . . . do you think He will condemn you for those transgressions . . .

The next time you have no food, . . . knock on the door of the church, . . . and if they are true, . . . they will give you food and shelter also, . . . but if they are false prophets, they will send you empty-away, . . . there is nothing wrong with the questions you raise, . . . as long as your heart is clean."

The woman nodded in agreement.

Joe looked across at the children, all of them except one, looking expectedly at him as if he was about to engage them in conversation, or play a game. And he saw at once that the girl, who had been sitting with down-cast eyes, and had been trying to hide her hare-lip, which he knew troubled her disfigured appearance. He smiled at her, but this only added to her embarrassment. The other children had been quietly watching and were aware that he had noticed her, and in her feelings of isolation she lowered her head further into her chest, he extended his outstretched arms in her direction, while the others waited and watched.

"Come to me," He said quietly.

She shook her head, and he could see the tears filling her eyes. He mother lifted her up and carried her to him, and he took her on his lap, as she struggled to hide herself from the others.

"Be still, . . . child, . . . I want to give you rest, . . ."

And he kissed the child on the lips, as a parent to a daughter, and handed her back to her mother, who thanked him for his kindness, but who then carried the weeping girl out of the veranda.

Other children stood up and went to him and touched him as if they anticipated something happening, for all of the mothers and older children there had become aware that something had changed in the room which had brought hope and a sense of relief, as if a heavy load had been lifted from the room and from their bodies. Some of the children came to him and told him their stories or sang to him, while others took his hand and turned it to examine its deep scar. They touched his face and his hair, as if in doing this brought them comfort; Connie watched this, also with a sense of interest and love. In her minds-eye she saw him walking in the Province, bringing hope and faith to the poorest families, and she saw herself as his handmaid, as if this moment was another version of a biblical story.

After the children had become settled again, some of the mothers came and sat at his feet and told him their problems, mainly about their poverty, but also about sickness, and about family problems, and drunken husbands, jealous neighbours, and exploitation from even the lowest petty officials who walk around demanding money from them for trumped-up offences, such as loitering or selling fruits in the street, or carrying something which looks like stolen goods. Where is the justice in this, they asked.

He answered them sometimes simply or with a parable, and he listened to their stories of how they try to balance the good with the bad in their ordinary lives.

One woman who had been standing back from the others, and holding a new-born baby came forward, with her many children.

"Sir, these are my children!"

They came and stood close to him, each one different in appearance, and he assumed that each child was of a different father.

"Where are their fathers ?" He asked.

The woman knew that he could see the differences in their faces, and that he might be considering her situation.

"Sir, all of these are street children, for I am barren, but God has given these children to me for my comfort, but this child here Sir, . . ."

She indicated a small sullen girl, a thin fragile child with the gait of an older woman.

"Sir, this girl is the mother of this baby, . . . she is not yet thirteen years Sir, . . . I saw her walking in the street, as I was going on the bus to Cavite Sir, . . . she was alone and walking bare-footed, . . . her body covered with dirt and dust, . . . her hair like a rag, . . . and heavily pregnant, . . . she was walking in the empty spaces between the buildings, . . . going nowhere Sir, . . . her face desolate, . . . even though I have nothing and no husband Sir, I brought her here, . . . she needs your blessing Sir."

He took the girls hand and looked into her face, which beneath the sadness of her eyes he noticed a pure and gentle childlike beauty, but he could see that she was burdened with the weight of her condition.

He said to her. "Talitha koum." which means—`little girl get up`.", and which Connie immediately remembered he had once said to her, but had not understood what it had meant then, or now.

He placed both hands on the girls head and closed his eyes and silently prayed.

For some reason Connie had identified herself with the girl, although she could not think why, and she had been carefully watching the girl, and as he removed his hands, the girl had changed; she now held her head erect—her dignity restored, and she smiled and took her small baby from the woman.

And to the woman he said.

"Do you not know, that whosoever shall receive one such little child in my name also receives me, . . . you will sit with me at the banquet, . . . you are the salt of the earth, . . . and those who afflict you will be afflicted."

At these words the woman also took on a renewed vigour and dignity, and returned to her place at the back of the veranda. But there was another woman with wild eyes who seemed to be unsettled and she had been haranguing some of the others, and she suddenly turned to him.

"Sir, . . . it is not fair that you ask us to abide by the commandments, and follow the laws, . . . when there are so many who abuse us, . . . even this morning a traffic police stopped me and emptied my bags, and would not let me go until I had paid him thirty peso, . . . is there a parable for that ?"

The woman stood waiting with her hands defiantly on her hips.

"You will be the one who tells the parable, and whatever you say will come to pass." He replied.

The woman thought for a moment, and then attempted to phrase her parable in what she imagined would be biblical terms.

"A certain woman went down to the market one morning, carrying her goods to sell, and before she entered the street where she set up her stall, a traffic cop made her empty her sack, and kicked her things into the puddles and the mud, and demanded a fine, for some imaginary offence, . . . his fine was thirty pesos, . . . the same payment as Judas Iscariot`s, and that was the total amount in my purse, . . . and he took it from me for his merienda, . . . but when he tried to buy, . . . the thirty pieces of silver had become hot like Daniel`s furnace and had melted into one small ingot, . . . and burned itself into his greedy palm, . . . Amen."

The woman's parable had struck a chord in the minds of the other women, who in a charitable act of solidarity all repeated her amen.

He remained seated drinking water that one of the women had brought, when the mother of the girl with the hare-lip quickly and breathlessly returned with her daughter.

"Sir, . . . Bless you Sir, . . . my daughter is cured, . . . look."

The remaining women closed in around them and peered at the daughter, scrutinising her mouth and letting out shrieks of surprise and delight.

"Its true Sir, . . . she is healed, . . . it was your kiss Sir, . . . Oh Hallelujah, . . ."

Some of the women became hysterical and started dancing and holding hands, and jumping up and down, their eyes bulging as if they had all imbibed exotic drugs.

Connie took his hand and drew him back along the corridor, to the comparative quietness of their rooms at the head of the village.

They sat in the small eating room and wedged the thin flap of a door against further attention.

"You see Connie, . . . they want everything to be miraculous, . . . and that is how they see it, . . . so that is how it is for them."

Connie had been trying to think how to protect him from their demands and enthusiasm, but she knew that whatever he said to them, they would interpret as miraculous and fantastic because she herself and her mother had the same yearnings.

"But it gives us hope, . . . and that is how we survive, . . . we live on hope !"

They both sat there in the small eating-room for a while saying nothing but silently thinking, when Ma. Theresa came in from the market looking flustered, and laden with vegetables and gossip.

"Sir Joe, . . . some of the stall-holders, . . . some who come from far way away, . . . but who know me, . . . were asking me about you Sir, . . . they were talking about miracles, . . . but I denied it, . . . because it might cause trouble Sir, . . . people here are jelly Sir, . . . and envious, . . ."

Conny and Joe exchanged glances, both knowing that sooner or later rumours would spread beyond the safe confines of the village and that there was nothing they could do about it to protect themselves from the poison of tsismis.

"This is the way of the world !" Joe said, and went to his room.

CHAPTER 25

During the next week the frenetic intrusions from the village women and children had subsided, and there were long periods of each day when he would stand motionless by the window as if hypnotised. Sometime Connie would pop her head in to see if he was available, but he was usually too intent to notice her, and sometime she would not disturb him, but one morning she had suddenly felt claustrophobic about staying indoors all the time for both of them and thought that it was a good time to entice him out of his cell and into the outside world of Quiapo.

She stood behind him humming a song to herself waiting for him to notice her, but he remained transfixed at the window for several minutes, then turned as if he had just awoken from his sleep; his expression a mixture of sadness and fear.

"Serenissima, . . . little one, . . . Connie, . . . I`m sorry, . . . I thought I saw the shadow of an angel`s wings against the blue-square of this small window, . . . beckoning me home, . . ."

He had spoken softly and intimately to her as if he was sharing a small personal secret, and she responded with a puzzled exptression on her face.

"What does it mean?" She asked.

He sat on the bed and she sat beside him before she realised their closeness.

"It means that soon my time will come!"

Connie was suddenly overcome with fear that something would happen and that Joe would either leave or be taken by someone or something beyond her understanding, and she grasped his hand in hers. He looked searchingly into her eyes, a look that she had seen several times before that now unsettled her with its intensity.

"Don't be afraid, . . . there is still time, . . . I will not leave you comfortless, . . . I will be with you always, . . . even if others cannot see me, . . . you will see and know that I am always with you!"

Connie's mind had flooded with confused thoughts, with too many questions, more than she knew how to ask, but most importantly she wanted to know what she should do now, for she already felt alone.

"But how will I learn, . . . just as I`m beginning to understand what you are telling me?"

"Connie, those women with their children have a simple faith, . . . for them that is enough, . . . and even for your mom, . . . but you, . . . you are curious and imagine there is something secret that you must know for you to be close to God, . . . let me tell you that you cannot know Him with your mind, . . . it is impossible, . . . that is not the way, . . . its the wrong direction, . . . its the reverse, . . . to learn how to empty your mind, . . . as you have already discovered, . . . it is not easy, . . . when you try to do this it is the worst of the contradictions I warned you about, . . . you see, . . . the harder we try to empty our mind the quicker our thoughts multiply, . . . and then we desperately feel the impossibility of finding Him, . . . and then the sudden darkness, like a cloud, . . . not a darkness of the night, but a darkness of not knowing, . . . yes, . . . cloud of unknowing between you and God, . . . which all must pass through if they are to truly come to know Him, . . . not as someone separate from themselves, . . . but as something interior, . . . deep within our souls, . . . to be mysteriously experienced in the deepest part of our being, . . . certainly it will terrify you the first time, . . . but then you have to be brave, . . . and abandon yourself, . . . Then eventually you will become One with Him, . . . and also, . . . One with Me."

His words were too heavy and too fast for her to take in; if only she had been able to write them down and work her way through them she knew that she would make sense of everything he had said, but his words danced in her mind, not as a single logical statement, but as phrases, and the final one, . . . to become one with god, . . . and also with him. The strange words embraced her like a forbidden lovers caress, knowing nothing of how close such feelings were to both the sensual and the mystical.

"Yes . . ." She said faintly . . . "I want that!"

But immediately she wanted to stop herself, to claw back those desperate words, knowing that he knew what was in her mind and her heart.

"Joe, . . . I have been thinking that it would be good if we could go out into the town, . . . and walk around and be among strangers, . . . for a change. I have never stayed indoors this long before, . . . we both need to get out, . . . and just walk around, . . . to feel the sun on our heads, . . . but you will need some shoes to protect your feet, . . . take your bath and I will go and buy for you, . . . will sports shoes be ok?"

She was back within an hour and they hurriedly got ready and went out into the bright sunlight.

CHAPTER 26

Connie had even bought him sunglasses, and as they strolled down towards Quiapo town centre; she felt for the first time a strange interest shown in her from passers-by. Not the usual kind of admiring glances she was accustomed to, but a resentful curiosity being with a foreigner. She could see that Joe was also aware of the hostile stares, and knew also that to other people walking past they must have looked like lovers or even worse, for Quiapo had its share of `hostesses`. Even with these thoughts in her mind she felt the pleasure of being alone with him, their arms linked, and she drank—in the warmth of the sun and the sense of open space as they approached the Plaza.

They stopped in the centre and looked around, turning in a circle as if pivoting on the centre of the square.

"What do you think? She asked.

Joe had been taking-in the different structures, looking up at the tall marble obelisk with its statue of a woman at its top with her outstretched arms welcoming him, and the huge bronze urns either side, and to one side what looked like a triumphal arch, which in his mind`s-eye re-located him somewhere in Roman times. As he turned around with the fierce sunlight flashes on his face, and its unaccustomed equatorial heat burning his exposed arms and head he felt himself spinning against the backdrop of the surrounding shops and the rear of the church, where people were sitting and standing and talking and moving, Connie felt him holding onto her as if he had lost his balance.

"Are you OK ?" She asked.

"Yes, it's the brightness of the sun I think, . . . its so bright here, but I'm OK, . . . we can walk around."

They skirted the plaza looking at the stalls of strange medicines; concoctions of all sorts in bottles and packets, and lucky charms and amulets, and crucifixes, and tiny colourful books of prayers, and crystals and statues of saints in garishly painted clothes intended to bring a little colour and light into peoples dull houses. He recognised some of the stall-holders as women and children from the village, and they greeted him with sheepish grins and hellos and offered him small gifts from their stalls.

"The market here sells everything anything anyone needs, . . . its all here." Connie said.

They strolled between the crowded stalls along one of the adjoining roads, meandering between the various sellers, of clothes, fruit, and other goods; the young stall-holders calling him to buy whatever they were selling, and calling out to him.

"Hey Joe, . . . come here Joe, . . . Gwapo Joe, . . ."

"Do you understand why they are calling you?" Connie asked.

Joe had been gripping her hand for comfort and protection.

"Yes, . . . I understand, . . . it is because I look different, . . . and maybe some think they know me, . . . is that right?"

"Partly !" She replied.

They walked back to the square, past the eateries and the fast-food outlets, and past the noisy masseurs and fortune-tellers and quack healers, all calling to them to use their services.

"Have you seen enough for now, or do you want to see inside the church ?"

He looked at her, although both of their eyes were shaded beneath the blank lenses of their sunglasses.

"It is a strange thing for you to ask." He said."

"But its here, . . . I would ask you the same if was a mosque or a Hindu temple, . . . its something to see, . . . and also for you to understand more why the women of simple faith can hope and survive, . . . and besides anything else, . . . this is the nearest they will ever get to seeing and knowing God".

He did not reply, but seemed to be contemplating her words, which had briefly reversed their roles; her the interpreter and he the listener. They veered towards the rear entrance and walked into the deep shade of the church to be confronted by the gory Santo Entierro—the larger than life effigy of the dead Christ lying in a magnificent glass coffin, with all of the vivid marks of his passion, and with an access hole at his feet permitting the faithful to touch his clay foot.

Together they waited and watched for a while the long line of waiting believers, as each one inserted their hand through the hole to touch the lifeless but lifelike representation of their Saviour, and he observed its effects; an overpowering ritualised effect which was also beyond his understanding, for he could now see for himself that these were simple acts by simple people yet miraculously making the spiritual for them, real.

They moved through the inner doors into the nave, and Connie guided him up to the transept so that she could show him the alter, with its giant statue of the Black Nazarene on His way to Calvary, surrounded by statues of the Blessed Virgin, and saints and angels. and to light a candle for her family in the province. Joe looked at everything as in a trance, his blank expression making it impossible for Connie to glean what sense he was making of it or what he was thinking. They both lit candles and Joe watched as Connie silently prayed. As they turned to walk away they were greeted by one of the priests who had been watching them and who was also a friend of Connie's family.

"Hello Connie, . . . so at last you have brought your visitor here, . . . I have been wondering when you might come, . . . we have heard so many things, . . . so its good to see you both."

Both of them were surprised by the priest's directness, but it was particularly alarming to Connie because she had been unaware of what rumours and gossip might have been carried into the church, and how the priests might react to Joe.

"Father, . . . this is Joe, . . . our visitor, . . ." Connie said.

"Yes Connie I know, . . . we heard that he has been about Our Lord's charitable work in your place, with the odd miracle thrown in for good measure."

The priest's terse comment struck Connie as confrontational, his welcome unfriendly.

She tried to steer Joe away, but she could feel his resistance, and thought for a moment that he might retaliate, but she also knew that they could not just escape for that might make matters worse, and besides she wanted to put things right for Joes sake.

"He is like you Father, . . . he is a man of God." She said defiantly but gently.

The priest had not expected this quick and challenging reply, especially as Connie had always been so shy when talking with him.

The priest scrutinised Joe`s face, narrowing his eyes as if dissecting each contour and line; his face was so close that he could have kissed him, then he said to Joe.

“Have you come to hinder us ?”

Joe stared back at him but said nothing.

Connie could see that the priest was shaking with frustration at Joe`s silence, and began nervously rolling his hands, one inside the other as if ritually washing them, then he said venomously.

“Do you know that if you had lived in the sixteenth century, when Christianity was brought here by the Spanish, . . . we would have burnt you for what you have done here, . . . go and come no more.”

Joe`s automatic response was to move his hand in front of the priest’s face, with his two fingers and thumb together as if holding an invisible communion wafer as if in a blessing.

The priest turned away, his eyes glaring angrily.

“Come, . . . let`s get out of here, . . . they’re all crazy here, . . .” Connie hissed.

They made their escape out of the side openings as if running from an enemy, and hurriedly made their way back to the village. Deciding between themselves that they would not mention the incident to the rest of the family.

Joe said that he needed to rest and went quietly to his room, but Connie felt that he had been wounded by the priest's sarcastic remarks. But she also needed time to think things over and to try to resolve some of the questions that she thought had been settled, but which now resurfaced with fresh implications and doubts and confusion.

She went to her tiny room and lay down on the mattress in the half-light, trying to clear her mind as Joe had suggested, but as she lay there clearing each little niggling question as it popped into her mind she was gripped by a sudden panic that she was going mad. She imagined that she was in a law court in a strange country, on trial for her beliefs and the prosecutors were hurling questions at her relentlessly. As each question was asked her mind raced to find an answer, but before she had time to answer, it was followed by another and another until she burst apart, torn to shreds, like the torn and lacerated back of someone who had been flagellated, her bare bleeding flesh exposed for all the Court to see. There were other prisoners waiting to be tried, among them Jose Rizal, or at least someone who resembled him.

She could see the black cloud above her separating her from the light which she knew was there, but denied her. She was hot, her clothes soaking wet with sweat, and she imagined her fever tipping her over the edge to insanity, into absolute despair, with a dull thudding sound in her head like the marching sound of an army. And then the sudden early morning cool breeze chilling her to the bone, and her interrogators still demanding answers to her question, her question, her question, . . . Connie do you believe?

A loud noise from outside woke her, and in her semi-conscious coming to, amidst her tumbling thoughts, she was back in her school class-room reciting to the whole class the final stanza from Rizal`s last poem before his execution, a poem she had chosen for her school project, and had also been required to memorise for her school exams:—

`Farewell, sweet stranger, my friend, who brightened my way:

Farewell to all I love. To die is to rest.`

She heard the sound of her mother in the small eating-room next door and the Easy Rock radio station blaring out its heart-felt message to Manila`s lonely hearts and lovers of Rock, and the comforting sounds of all the families noisily cooking and eating and talking.

CHAPTER 27

Early the following morning Ma. Theresa heard the first rumblings of trouble as she walked down the long narrow passage-way at the heart of the village, picking up snippets of rumours from some of the mothers and their children, who worked in the market. From what she could make-out, some of the priests in the church had become curious and angry about the man who was claiming that he had risen from the dead.

As soon as she had dealt with some of the other earthly problems, she hurried back to her kitchen to share her news with her husband and any of the other Councillors, and as she had expected, some of them were already gathered there discussing the matter.

"So you know also husband ?" She asked.

The Barangay Captain looked worried, and led the small group into the small council office.

"Yes, it could be more serious than the attack, . . . because if the priests accused them of meddling in religious matters, especially as they had not reported the dead body and doing heretical things, . . . there was no knowing what the authorities would do, . . . because the church had more power than anyone, . . ."

They all agreed with him, but were more frightened than usual because of the arcane mechanisms of the church which were secret and mysterious, and could bring the village down because of the power of politicians and business-people and lawyers and judges, and even the President, and because they would have the sympathy of the ordinary people. Counsellor Pepe, who always wished to pronounce his thoughts as if it was an official edict chimed in.

"Yes," He said. "This is so, so very very, . . . serious, that if they played it their way, then they could burn us out and nobody would criticise them, . . . they would say, . . . it`s an Act of God, . . . and nobody would do anything to help us."

They sat quietly mulling it over then the Barangay Captain said.

"We don`t know what they think, . . . and we`re stupid really to think that we could keep it a secret, . . . as far as we`re concerned we have not done anything wrong, . . . but that`s not how they`ll see it, . . . my main concern, . . . at this time, . . . is the protection of the village, . . . we will have to move him, . . . in case they come here, . . . looking for him, . . . we don`t know what they want, . . . yet."

Ma. Theresa had been listening attentively and reluctantly agreed with her husband. The other Counsellors agreed, and started discussing other business and drinking their coffee.

Ma. Theresa called Connie and quickly told her about the short counsellors meeting and of their decision.

"So where will he go Mom?" She asked, looking worried.

"We can think about it and ask Joe, . . . we can explain things, . . . even its embarrassing but he will understand it, . . ."

They prepared breakfast together and called Joe to eat.

Connie had decided that it was their visit to the church had probably sparked things off, and that the situation was partly her fault.

"Joe, . . . the priest yesterday is curious about you, . . . and dad and mom and the counsellors think it is dangerous if you stay here, . . . and as it is nearly All Souls day, it wont look suspicious if we take you to the province, . . . but not our usual province, . . . and then we can find you somewhere safe, . . . so we need to prepare quickly, . . . is that ok?"

Joe had already overheard some of the gossip from the solitude of his small room, and could sense and anticipate their need for him to move somewhere.

Ma. Theresa called Peter and Johnny and explained the problem and asked if they could come home early so that the family could plan what to do, and her husband organised transportation with one of his reliable contacts, and by the time the two brothers arrived, all was ready. They had packed a few clothes and the evening meal was already cooked, but they said nothing to anyone, even their closest neighbour.

They ate their food quietly with the radio on full-blast to drown-out anything they might let slip, as if participating in a conspiracy. As they finished their meal, one by one they let themselves out of the side-door and individually walked to the end of the street to avoid anyone seeing them getting into the small van; Pepi had insisted that it must be regarded the same as a `military operation`, and that they had to just disappear into the night, and head north to Pangasinan, or Ilocos or even further.

They drove through the night, stopping at small all-night eateries, Joe remaining inside the van, and as the sun came up they passed through Urdeneta, and along quiet deserted highways, until they reached an isolated farm shack, occupied by Ma. Theresa`s relatives. They hurriedly unloaded the van and let the driver return to Manila, and they set about organising themselves. They had brought rice and fish with them, and Ma. Theresa and her relatives busied themselves with the breakfast.

Joe was introduced as a new friend of Connie's, a tourist who would be going onto the mountain region alone, so all the others politely ignored him as nobody special.

In another two days it would be `All Souls` night, but they had not yet decided where they would celebrate it; this part of Pangasinan was familiar territory and there were several places where they could pay their respects to the departed.

In the meantime there were no immediate pressures and they could plan suitable locations where Joe could stay without attracting too much attention.

The farm was far from any barangays and was isolated and never visited by anyone; the land was poor for growing anything, and the nearest river was also far away. Her relatives grew vegetables and had planted a few fruit trees, and had constructed a primitive irrigation trench, but to grow rice they needed more regular irrigation and also fertiliser, as the soil seemed to be exhausted.

Joe and Connie walked across the fields enjoying the freedom of its openness and chatted casually about the previous day and about the momentum of the situation that had brought them so quickly to the farm.

"Are you worried ?" Joe asked.

"Slight, . . . its just that anyone can stir-up trouble here, sometimes unintentionally, . . . and one thing leads to another, . . . and before you know it, . . . its a crisis . . . and if you're not there it will probably die-down and be forgotten in a week, . . . but I think its safer for you to stay away for a while."

Joe nodded and asked her if they were going to leave him there.

"Its up to you." She replied. "But its easier if you are in the south, . . . in Cavitie because my brods are there and they can keep an eye on things, . . . and they`re smart and they will know how to look after you, . . . and they like you, . . . so you have your family there, . . . and we can keep in touch."

He smiled at this and reached out to take her hand.

"Be careful they might be watching us." She said quickly.

They walked to the edge of the field, standing in the shadow of a tree both silently watching someone in the distance breaking the hard soil, their solitary silhouette mechanically repeating over and over their movements, swinging a hammer-like implement; a relentless ritual in obeisance to the rice-god.

"Did you know, . . . I had a fever after our trip to town ?" Connie asked.

"Connie, . . . I could sense it, . . . it had to be, . . . that was the real crisis, . . . the battle between your head and your heart, . . ."

"But before that, . . . I thought I had understood, . . . and that I was certain, . . . but you are right Joe, . . . my mind was playing tricks, . . . I`m still not sure, . . ."

She continued looking across the field to avoid confronting his gaze.

"Connie, listen to me carefully, . . . I must tell you this, . . . you must hold onto your doubts also, . . . do you know those words, . . . `for the devil walketh about seeking all whom he may devour, ` . . . honest doubt is part of true faith, . . ."

She understood.

"But now I`m thinking all the time about what will happen, . . . to you, . . . and to me . . . I`m trying to think how we will work it out, . . . you would`nt survive if we left you here, . . . look at this farm, . . . the people here are my moms relatives, . . . so very poor and with nothing, . . . its a wasteland, . . . a desert, . . . where the sun beats down, . . . and hardly any trees for shelter, . . . and no water."

Joe`s eyes flashed in a way she had come to know when he was challenged.

"But they survive Connie, . . . they continue, . . . they have children and they care for their parents, . . . they are destitute but not deserted, . . . they are part of the history of the world, . . ."

"Yes I know, . . . but even a few days ago, . . . their new baby died of dehydration, . . . because they could not afford one single bottle of saline-solution, . . . maybe three or four hundred pesos would have saved their baby, . . . and they had to wait and watch their beautiful daughter die, . . . and even more tragic, . . . my cousin made a small casket for the baby, and before they closed it, they wanted a picture for remembrance, . . . but nobody they knew owned a camera, . . . so even their remembrance was denied them, . . . that is how hard it is for them Joe, . . . and for many here."

As she spoke, without knowing them, he was visualising their sorrow, and could share for each one of them, their anguish and pain.

"Connie, . . . there is a time for all of us to weep, . . . our times of joy and despair are like the seasons, . . . after the harvest everything dies, . . . and as the Spring rains refresh the dry earth there is renewal, . . . new life, . . . that is the pattern, the rhythm of the poetry of existence, . . . that is God`s promise of eternal return, . . . we are all part of that promise, . . . how could it be otherwise?"

Connie felt the strength of his words, . . . not only as an explanation of why things should be as they are, but also as a personal and intimate reassurance of his love. She felt relieved that they had been able to spend a little time together, and he surprised her further by reflecting her private and personal whimsical thoughts. As they walked back to the family he said.

"Now you have seen Connie, . . . even in this barren place there is new life, . . . this too is reincarnation, . . .

They walked round to the back of the house, where her family were gathered, sitting in the shade of the rusting corrugated shack, chatting with their cousins and cutting vegetables, with the children, their skin darkened by the sun, played in the dry dust, while the wild chickens disappointedly scratched the surface for sustenance. Connie and Joe sat quietly with them and listened to episodes of their trials and tribulations and small and infrequent triumphs and constant disasters. But even in their poverty there were smiles and laughter, and it was this that lifted Connie's mood and made her happy and at peace with herself.

It had been a whole year since Ma. Theresa had seen her cousins and there was a whole year`s family life to catch up on. Lunch flowed into dinner, and the supplies of meat and fish they had brought with them had become an essential part of the yearly ritual of renewal and reminiscing and remembrance. They decided that they would celebrate `All Saints` and `All Souls` Days at Asingan, Ma. Thersa`s birthplace and also the resting place of her parents and other departed family members.

CHAPTER 28

The following day both families rode into Asingan sitting in another relative`s farm-trailer pulled by a tractor-like vehicle; and for most of the day Ma. Theresas family visited; scattered relatives, the market, attended mass in the church, and stopped in the road whenever someone called out to them. Joe was always included in any reunions and quickly learned what was expected of him when meeting other members of the family and old friends, and gradually pieced together the immense puzzle of Pinoy family life. And also learned of the many ways that his presence could be accounted for; he was sometimes a stranger, a family friend, a helper, a teacher, etc, etc., and wherever they went he was always embraced and welcomed.

Even in the crowded church he could feel the warmth of their acceptance and friendship and in their celebration of their mass with its essence of eternal reoccurrence, and he could see in all of their faces, expressions of openness and fellowship and kindness. The whole space inside was full, families with their children, most of them in holiday-mood, but some in their working clothes, and all at one point embracing each other in the sharing of `the Peace`, although he was an unknown visitor and a stranger, he had the feeling that he knew them all, and that all of them knew him.

That night the whole family slept together on the floor of a relative's house, and the following day began with prayers around a simple family shrine, with fading photographs of parents and others, and small flickering candles, and a small collection of figurines of saints and crucifixes.

The whole family could see that Connie was once again relaxed, and always at Joe`s side as his guide and companion as they prepared for their all-night vigil in the cemetery. They prepared and cooked their food for the night-time, and took blankets and candles and set-off for the cemetery, which by night-fall was already alive with families assembled round the graves and tombs sheltering beneath their make-shift canopies, huddling together in the candle-light.

Ma. Theresa`s family-tomb had been cleaned and repainted, and Peter and Johnny had carried some wooden planks with them which they used to form a bench. Each held a candle as they waited for the priest who was going about, from family group to family group and starting them off with their prayers and blessing them. Ma. Theresa started them singing the `Ave`, and they settled into a circuit of prayers, one for each name on the family tomb. And as the cemetery filled up with more families the whole place came alive with clusters of candle-light and with the mixed sounds of singing and the recitation of prayers, and sounds of weeping and pitiful cries of loss.

Joe was also meditating and deep in silent prayer as Connie edged closer to him for comfort. She pulled her blanket around both of their shoulders, and in the half-light they appeared to the others as belonging to each other.

Each family group had its own schedule with interludes for snacks and reminiscences between the prayers and hymns, and once in a while someone could be heard comforting another and the night of all-souls was filled with the wishes and hopes for the peaceful repose of the departed souls and for the hoped-for resurrection.

Connie whispered into Joe`s ear.

"What will the resurrection and the last day of Judgement be like."

He took her hand in his underneath the blanket and started to tell her, sometimes whispering and other time shaping the sounds carefully with his mouth.

"It will be even more frightening than as it is written in the Book of Revelation. For there will be armies of angels and the sounds of many trumpets, and the frightened cries of multitudes, and the separation of those who are rejected and those who are invited to the wedding banquet for the marriage for the Lamb and His wife, and She will be ready, arrayed as a saint in pure and clean white linen, and all shall celebrate the new heaven and the new earth, and so all will begin again as I have told you, . . . and the Lamb, the Son of Man will show His bride to all who will celebrate their marriage, . . . a marriage in and of heaven and earth, and there will be no more death, for the former things are passed away."

Connie could feel the pulse of his hand in hers, and the rhythm of his words, and felt the power and strength of His presence.

"And will that be the end of time?" She asked.

"Yes." He said, "That will be the final word, . . . at that moment all will be resolved, . . . and what follows will be Eternity!"

After he had finished speaking Connie wanted to continue the conversation, but she couldn't speak, for as each new question formed in her mind it instantly dissolved as if everything she could have asked had already been answered. And when her Mom called her it was as if she was returning from a distant place.

As the sun came up, all of the groups were still huddled together, their blankets damp with dew, and the deafening sound of roosters crowing bringing a new day.

During the morning they decided that the best solution was for Joe to lodge for a while with the two brothers in one of the cheap boarders` houses in Rosario, along the coast of Cavite where there were many small businesses connected with the fishing trades, and where there were large numbers from the provinces who were temporary employees, where he would be one stranger among many. They would travel during the night and arrive there too early in the morning to attract attention from anyone. Connie was apprehensive but was assured by her brothers and her Mom that Joe would be cared for and protected.

They travelled by bus to Cavite and by jeepney to Rosario and installed themselves in one of the anonymous cheap one-room lodging houses in a dusty side street, with barely enough room for the bed-spacers double-decker bunk, the CR, and a small cooking space with a narrow sink, all with just about enough space for three adult males. But the best thing about it was its communal atmosphere with its tacit agreement that all should live and let live, and not interfere with anything. For most of the time Peter and Johnny would be working at one of the boatyards building and repairing boats, so for most of the day Joe would be alone.

For the first few days Joe remained inside the small room where the two brothers took it in turn to cook and prepare his food and attend to his other needs, but he soon felt uncomfortable with this arrangement, and as soon as they left for work in the morning he would stroll along the sea-front where the various fish factories processed fish one way or another. He walked between the boat yards, where the fishing boats were repaired and where the nets were hung out to dry and made ready for the next trip. And the sea breeze carried the smells of fish and smoke into his nostrils, and he felt the comfort of fellowship with the fishermen and the boatmen, most of whom were there to earn money for their families who were scattered among the provinces. But one morning as he was preparing to go out, there was a knock on the door, and he waited silently to be left alone, but then another knock, and Connie`s voice calling him to open up.

Once inside she greeted him, and without restraint, she wrapped her arms around him, and drew herself close to him.

"I`ve missed you, . . . I`m so lonely." She shouted,

"And I prayed for you to come back, . . . and my mom, . . . nothing has happened there, . . . and everyone says they miss you, . . . but I needed to see you, . . . to be with you, . . . my mom knows I`m here, . . . even we're alone, . . . is it ok for you?"

He smoothed her hair from her face and kissed her forehead the way her father did.

"Yes it`s lonely here, . . . for me too, . . . without you I feel exiled, . . . imprisoned, . . . so each morning I seek solace along the beach, . . . and sometimes I look across the Bay trying to locate your whereabouts, . . . I always think of you . . . we fit together like the wings of a prayer, . . . little Serenissima—I call you this, . . . did you know that it means . . . `mother of tomorrow`, . . . thank you for your prayers, . . . for me, . . . they are sighs in the darkness of eternity."

"Can I stay here with you, . . ." She asked softly, burying her head in his chest. "But I have to return home before dinner, . . . I promised my mom."

He held her at first as if she was a child, and then as a woman; neither of them finding the words to say what it was they were feeling for fear of what might happen.

By the time her brothers returned she had prepared their food, and she had explained how she needed to see them, and that her mom had agreed that it was OK. and that they could trust her, and that she was worried and needed to talk with him.

When it was time for her to go, her brods left them alone so that they could spend a few minutes together in private. They immediately reached out for each other gripping and holding each other, she brushing her face against his, and he capturing her essence in the scent of her breath.

In this last embrace at the end of her visit it seemed to both of them that they had arrived at a different point in their lives, and that time itself had played some trick with them, catapulting them into the future, as if they had been together for a lifetime. And when they quickly shared their last thoughts, his replies came to her questions in her head without anything passing his lips, and he also knew her thoughts, such was their compatibility and agreement about the world and all that was in it.

CHAPTER 29

Over following few days Peter, Johnny and Joe became brothers, sharing the chores and their troubles and concerns, and through their conversations, especially when discussing relationships, it became obvious that Joes and Connie's friendship was deepening.

Whereas before, Peter and Johnny had seen Joe as `distant, ascetic, and aloof, they now found him brotherly and caring, and with an unusual sense of humour and child-like curiosity. They joked with him about his apparent shyness and hinted at his `sweetness` for their sister, although he was not sure what this meant. And they talked about their futures and their girl-friends, and marriage and about the `accident` that had brought him to the village and into their family.

They asked him about his wounds and how they had happened, and about his roots, and his birthplace, and accepted without question what he told them; that he didn't know. And they came to trust one another, and when occasionally Peter or Johnny called home, they would hand him their cell-phones to say a few words to Connie.

And they told him about their work repairing and building fishing boats and about Fiestas and Celebrations, and that as Babylon did not actually occupy any land and so could not legally claim a title as a Barangay, or celebrate its own Saints day or enjoy its own Fiesta, instead it had to share the Fiestas of others`; the Fiesta of the Black Nazarine in Quiapo, and the Flores de Mayo, Santacruzan, and the celebration of Porta Vaga, here in Rosario which they knew about and had participated in as Marshalls helping to launched the floating shrine carrying the image of Our Lady of Solitude into waters of Manila Bay, to be steered across the Bay, honouring Her patronage and protection.

"You must come with us, . . . you will love it, . . . lots of people, . . . and excitement, . . . and Connie and all of us will be there."

The thought of being included in celebrations as part of the family enthralled him, and immediately agreed. The real excitement of this ceremony, they told him was the launching of the floating shrine from one of the piers, after it had been carried through the town.

"You will be with us, and you can feel the happiness, like energy filling your body, . . . if you have any illness it disappears." Johnny said.

"And marching bands and dancers, and a procession all the way through the town, . . . of my word, . . . you`ll love it." Peter added.

Carried away by the anticipated excitement, they described the various fiestas they had enjoyed since their childhood, and how they were the mile-stones in their lives.

CHAPTER 30

On the Saturday evening before the Fiesta Connie called her brothers and asked to speak to Joe.

"I hope you are well Joe, . . . we will see each other tomorrow, . . . I`m so excited, . . . missed you so much."

Her words were no longer those of a girl, but of a woman who needed to express her feelings.

"Same here." He replied.

"Whats your feelings now?" She asked.

"You know it." He said.

"It would be nice if you tell me how much."

There was a slight laughter in her voice which made him smile.

"You know that also, . . . but if you want my words, . . . you will be my love for eternity."

"Wow!" She gasped.

"See you tomorrow then, . . . bye"

With her words ringing in his ears he returned to discussing the fiesta.

On the morning of the ceremony the boatyard workers and fisherman's wives set out to decorate the newly painted palanquin with flowers and braids, with the image of Our Lady of Porta Vaga fastened beneath the small dome. They speculated on how rough the weather across the bay had been recently and how the swimmers who propelled the palanquin would need to take extra care.

Peter and Johnny dressed in their Marshals shirts took Joe to the church where the palanquin-shrine was to be blessed by the Bishop, and waited to see their mom and dad and Connie, but they had not arrived, and once the blessing had been completed, they would have to walk with the Palanquin, keeping the way clear so the procession does not lose its momentum. Joe walked with them, keeping his eye on them and following their directions.

School Bands in ceremonial uniforms headed the gathering procession, followed by troupes of dancers, who could`nt wait for things to get started and were swaying in the usual way when parading along the route. The bands started playing, and the dancers started their lilting waltz-like zigzagging dance, from one side of the street to the other, the crowd moved in, and drummers and majorettes and cheer-leaders joined in where there was a gap, and slowly the procession moved along the street, the many Bearers carrying the heavy white construction on their shoulders, also swaying in rhythm to the drum-beat, and moving slowly towards the quay from where they would launch it into the sea.

Joe was unable to resist the enchantment of the drum-beat, and without realising it had become part of the swaying crowd, which was now like a mythical creature progressing along its ordained route with one single aim, which was to launch the palanquin to regenerate the covenant with Our Lady of Porta Vaga and honour her patronage, and he was being carried irresistibly along with it.

Finally they were there and he found himself being pulled by the Bearers and the Marshals along the side of the pier, as the heavy palanquin was being carefully manoeuvred to the edge ready for launching, when a sudden powerful squall lifted the palanquin out of the grips of the men leaning over the side of the pier. At that point it was pandemonium; shouting and screaming and bodies jumping into the water reaching up to steady it, and at one point when it suddenly shifted and began to slide, many hands reaching out to hold and steady it. In their excitement some of the youths jumped in and began playfully slapping the water, shooting fine sprays over those on the pier and for a few minutes the water around the bobbing palanquin became a torrent of eddies, heads bobbing under the water to re-emerge on the other side, while those watching from the small boats began singing hymns, and one of the officiating priests confusedly delivering the departing prayer. Then Peter who was in the water was gripped by a sudden panic; in that mad heaving moment when the shrine almost capsized, he had lost contact with Joe, and was now desperately calling his name and searching for him among the torrent of bodies; those still on the pier and others in the water also looked round for Joe, but he was nowhere in view. He called to the others, checking for a sight of Joe, some of the boats were beginning to move away, and some of the youths were swimming towards the shore. Peter dived beneath the Palanquin but it all was clear, then someone was shouting from the pier and pointing at a brown patch in the water behind them. A body was floating face-down with blood oozing from its side, its arms outstretched, and instantly Peter knew it was Joe.

The Palanquin was being propelled by swimmers, and already out of reach. Other swimmers moved towards the body trying to hold it but the sea suddenly shook, like a quake, and the frightened swimmers either clung to the metal pilings of the pier or slashed their way to the few boats. Peter pulled himself up out of the water shaking his head at Johnny.

"He`s gone!" He gasped. "I don`t know what we can do now, . . . it was so quick, . . . he`s lost."

They both knew that swimmers had often drowned before in previous years, in the same way that pilgrims were annually crushed during the festival of the Black Nazareno, but now they were bereft, wondering how they could tell Connie.

Dark clouds had formed over the Bay, and torrential rain brought the celebrations to a swift close as the main street flooded. And the Palanquin had to be rescued before it reached the shore. There was nothing they could do to retrieve the body as none of the boatmen were willing to help.

The typhoon continued throughout the night and the following day, flooding the roads and stopping the bus services to Manila, preventing the two brothers from going home. There were continuous brownouts and the telephone signals had collapsed, with occasional opportunities to contact the rest of the family.

Nothing moved until midweek, when at last the storm abated and the buses returned to service. They arrive back home dejected and desolate, and could hardly bear greeting Connie, who was distraught but placid, her appearance changed and womanly.

Their mothers face was distorted with grief, in a way they had never seen before; her strong voice choked with incessant sobs, and their dad, dazed and harrowed.

"It was the storm !" Peter said.

"There had been no warning, just a little rough water, but no signs of a storm." Johnny added.

They were all packed into the small eating room, remembering the last time they had all eaten there together, the time when Joe had become truly part of their family. They held hands round the table and prayed for his soul, but Connie could not find the words, and gently let herself out of the room. And later Ma Theresa prepared dinner, and called Connie to come and eat, but there was no reply.

They looked into her room, but she was not there, and again they panicked, thinking that she might do something in her grief. As they passed-by the small room they saw her lying on his bed, not sleeping but quietly whispering. They let her be.

The following morning Connie was awake early, telling the enquiring mothers and children that Joe had gone home, but that he would come again, . . . sometime.

EPILOGUE

To the authorities Babylon was too frequently depicted as the exemplary slum, with the highest concentration of social problems and criminals; but actually there was more social cohesion and harmony locked into that one place than might be found in any of the surrounding barangays, and as for criminality, the only arrests there were those set-up by the police who needed the occasional easy target. There were also fewer cases of domestic violence, less shootings, less fights, less stealing, and fewer family feuds.

So the following Easter when the usual small number of schoolgirls and unattached young women announced that they were with child, there was the usual response, and the only surprise this time was the inclusion of Connie, Ma Theresa`s talented daughter, on the list. Unbelievably, not only because she was the daughter of the strictest mother in Babylon, and most probably in the whole of Manila, or because she was the most talented, most beautiful, and most graceful, but because Connie was seen by all the other families and their daughters as virginal and untouchable, a paragon of virtue, and outstandingly smart. But now surprisingly she was pregnant, and the one question on everyone's lips was, who had fathered her child?

As soon as her bump became noticeable there began the usual mild questions and insinuations and jokes, because none of the family really believed that it could be possibly true. And when asked, she simply smiled and lowered her gaze! But as her pregnancy became increasingly obvious, each member of her family engaged her in their own form of interrogation. They asked who, how, and when; and what were they to do about it? Her mother became frantic with fear, wailing with pain and suggesting that an immediate marriage would be necessary, her father was dumbfounded but tried to keep the peace, and her eldest brother swaggered around swearing to kill the guy who had shamed his family. There were many family discussions, and possible culprits identified, but Connier refused to discuss the matter; not even when or how it had happened. None of the family had suspected it, for she had never shown any interest in boys which led the family to suspect rape, but this too seemed impossible as she seemed so serene and quietly happy with her condition.

As the months passed she silently busied herself with some of the domestic chores in the kitchen which she had rarely done before, and at odd moments she would stand at the small windows in the small room that had been Joes, her vacant gaze fixed as if expecting someone or something. She had changed with her pregnancy, from being the vivacious young student to someone self-absorbed to the point of self-sufficiency. And she remained so until her time was due.

Connies's contractions started during the night of Easter Sunday, they were so mild that her mother anticipated a long wait, but on Monday morning everything happened very quickly. Half the family was out at church and her mother who had been preparing breakfast, asked one of the nurses if they should go to hospital, but it was already too late, the contractions quickened and the nurse delivered the baby.

Instead of the expected familiar brown skin and the families` features, the baby was pale with Joe`s blue eyes and high nose. Her mother gasped, trying to unravel in her mind how this could be? As far as she knew the two of them had never been left to themselves, and surely Joe would not have taken advantage of someone so young, . . . and impossible to think that Connie would have coupled with the quiet contemplative monk-like stranger. Not in a million years, no not possible, she was turning her thoughts over and over in her troubled mind. Trying to control her panic! She was crying loudly, "Not Joe! Not Connier! Not humanly possible, . . . No, No, No."

Sobbing and swaying as if delirious, and trying to hold onto to the belief that this was not really happening, but must be a kind of hallucination, a nightmare even. Her mind was on fire; images of the past year danced into focus and then evaporated, something was lifting her, easing her off from where she stood, it felt as if she was about to fly, all she needed to do was to extend her arms and she would be carried away, and then the strange sudden feeling of contentment, as she took the baby from the nurse.

During the previous few weeks Connie had chosen to sleep in Joe`s room because of the heat, and with its single small window it was cooler, and she had been sleeping on the same low bamboo bed; his bed which had witnessed his resurrection. A sudden wild thought occurred to Ma. Theresa; surely it's possible that this could be the explanation? After all, Joe was not like any other man she had known, they all knew he was different; it must be possible, and in a moment the thought became fact. After all, she told herself, things like this had happened before; she knew a girl who had once given birth to a white baby without even seeing a foreigner, and that was because she had paid her devotions to the pale statue of Santo Niño in her room, and that was an indisputable fact. She had seen the baby and it had the same smile as the boy-saint`s statue. But how could she convince others about Connie`s baby?

Although Ma. Theresa was an ardent Catholic some of her attitudes were more those of a Buddhist. Certainly she lived her life, not in the past or the future, but totally grounded in the present, in the `here and now`, so when this wild, and almost preposterous thought suddenly occurred to her, the palpitations immediately ceased, and it seemed to her that no further explanation was necessary. She also decided at the next moment that she would say nothing of these thoughts, but continue to care for her daughter as if nothing untoward had happened. As if all that had happened had been for a purpose!

And that was also how the family, and eventually her near neighbours, and in the fullness of time, how all of those who dwelt in Babylon, came to see it and accept it, because eventually it was everyone's story. But it was these fragments of Connie`s reminiscences and reflections of how the man, they all knew as Joe, but whom she alone knew as Son of

Man, had changed all of their lives, with a promise which she carried in her heart, and which sustained her in her moments of doubt and loneliness, and which she repeated to herself and recited to her daughter as a talisman of consolation and hope.

To the families residing in Babylon the naming of a child is a serious business; although there are occasional disasters, where the parents are unaware of the connotations of a name, and are attracted only by the sound of it, or what they take to be it`s meaning. Consequently many unfortunate children are named in the exaggerated hope that the magical elements of their name will bring them fame and fortune. This was also Ma. Theresa`s view, believing that the special circumstances of her granddaughters birth should be celebrated by being awarded the name of one her favourite saints, but Connie announced that it had already been decided, at the moment of conception! Theresa was slightly shocked when she heard this, imagining that there must have been something like a pact or a covenant between her daughter and Joe, which suggested to her then that their coupling had been more frequent than she had previously thought, especially if they had found time to speculate on the question of the child's name. And in fact this was partly true, for Joe had enchanted Connie with his stories, which she took to be predictions, and which always included their unborn daughter, who he described as Semiramis. Connie recalled that when he spoke like that it sometimes sounded like another enigma or riddle which she needed him to explain.

"Yes, Connie, you should become acquainted with Semiramis, for she was the first queen of Babylon, . . . her name means gift of the sea, . . . and also she was to become the original queen of heaven, . . . who now resides in the milky way as a star, but will once again become mortal when your time is due, . . . look at the northern sky and you will see her."

If Connie had dared to share more of these secret moments with her mother at that time, although Ma. Theresa would have found it difficult to understand them, she at least would have been able to appreciate Connie`s strange exotic choice of the name-Semiramis, and her love for the story-teller.

Lightning Source UK Ltd.
Milton Keynes UK
UKOW040702131012

200526UK00001B/14/P

9 781477 237885